Ann Summers

Madame B's
White Hot & Wild Whispers

Ann Summers

Madame B's
White Hot & Wild Whispers

EBURY
PRESS

1 3 5 7 9 10 8 6 4 2

Published in 2007 by Ebury Press, an imprint of Ebury Publishing

Ebury Publishing is a division of the Random House Group

Text written by Siobhan Kelly © Ebury Press 2007

The Random House Group Limited Reg. No. 954009

Addresses for companies within the Random House Group can be found at
www.randomhouse.co.uk

A CIP catalogue record for this book
is available from the British Library

The Random House Group Limited makes every effort to ensure that
the papers used in our books are made from trees that have been
legally sourced from well-managed and credibly certified forests. Our
paper procurement policy can be found on www.randomhouse.co.uk

Printed in the UK by CPI Cox & Wyman, Reading, RG1 8EX

ISBN: 9780091916466

CONTENTS

FOREWORD

Welcome to Ann Summers' new collection of erotic short stories, a new and thrilling series destined to become essential bedtime reading.

I'm really excited to be able to bring you these ten tales of women who boldly go wherever their desires take them. We know that our customers are the sexually confident, fabulous women who love sex and aren't afraid to show it.

From the no-holds-barred stories to the gentle and romantic, I promise that this collection of erotic tales has something for each and every one of you. So without any further ado, I hand you over to our narrator, the mysterious Madame B . . .

Jacqueline Gold

Dear Reader,

Welcome to book number two of Madame B's erotic tales:
bedtime stories that will have you doing anything but
sleeping! I collect other women's sexual confessions: true
stories from ladies who have taken a walk on the sexual
wild side, and want to share their sizzling secrets.

For years, I have written these titillating tales in a
red leather notebook that I carry with me all over the
world and read whenever I want to lose myself in a
steamy story. But the contents of that notebook are so
sexually intense it seemed a shame not to share them
with a wider audience.

Since I published my first volume of true confessions,
I've been busy gathering new stories to feed the public's
appetite for the truth about what everyday, ordinary women
(and at least one globally renowned female) really get up
to. So here it is – another collection of arousing, astonish-
ing stories from women who've taken their sexual fantasies
to the limit and fulfilled their orgasmic potential. Some of

their stories are soft and romantic; some are shocking and hardcore. All of them really happened.

So the only question now is . . . which one's your favourite?

Happy reading,

Madame B x

VELVET UNDERGROUND

Who hasn't fantasised about a stranger on a train to make the daily commute go by that little bit quicker? There's something so highly charged about two unfamiliar bodies, both on different journeys, united in ecstasy for a few minutes and then going their separate ways again . . .

But would you ever make it happen? The girl who told me this story didn't think she was the kind to take those sort of risks in public – but that was before she found herself alone, in a tunnel, with a tall, handsome stranger.

When I was a little girl in the Home Counties suburbs, I found riding the London Underground an enormous treat, an exotic, exciting experience when on occasional trips with my parents to the capital. I watched in awe the sophisticated, sexy women and smart, handsome men who travelled on it. I loved the mysterious, evocative names of the stations ('Angel', 'Seven Sisters' and 'Elephant & Castle' sounded to me like characters from a fairy story and I really did expect to see clowns and a lion tamer at Piccadilly and Oxford 'Circuses') and the swarming labyrinths packed with bodies all underneath the streets of London – anything could happen in a place like this.

And now that I'm twenty-five, and living in London, and I make the same journey on the same Tube train every day, what does the Tube mean to me? Boredom, routine and frustration, that's what. And it makes me sad that I'd totally lost my childlike fondness for it and a thrill for the speed and sound. I'm on it for thirty minutes, twice a day: the once exotic Underground has become a symbol of humdrum working life where each weekday is the same. My fellow commuters are the same every day: like me, they line the platforms at exact spots, all the better to access the seat they want on their preferred carriage. I know which points on the line are likely to get signal failure and stop in a tunnel for five minutes with no warning or explanation; I know the section of the track where the train rattles suddenly downhill or swings abruptly to one side. All in all, it's a predictable, mechanical place: hardly the most likely location for the most intense, charged sexual experience of my life.

It was a midsummer evening, that time of year when there's still daylight until about 9 p.m. I didn't get away from work till 10 o' clock, and when I made my way to the platform, it was half-deserted: too late for the commuter rush, too early for chucking-out time. I had the carriage to myself: once in, I pulled down the window, letting the dirty zephyr that swept through the carriage gently wipe the dew of perspiration off my lip and collar-bone. I raised my arms above my head, grateful for the cooling breeze of the light wind on my hot skin. Then I sank on to a hard, scratchy chair and tried to relax. Not for the first time, I noticed how the easy vibrations of the train had a gentle massaging effect on every part of my body. Double-checking that no one could see, I crossed my legs and rocked back and forth a little to enhance that sensation. Look, it was hot, I was horny and I hadn't had sex for ages: a girl's got to get her cheap thrills wherever and however she can, right? I closed my eyes and squeezed my legs together, feeling the blood rush to my pussy. I was surprised how quickly mild arousal built up a head of steam. 'I could actually make myself come,' I thought, as the train rattled along, pleasantly jolting and jerking my body around. 'If I just slip my hands down my panties and help finish this, I could bring myself off right here.'

As soon as the thought occurred, I knew I'd have to do the deed. I'm not normally reckless, and certainly not given to public masturbation, but something took over that night – call it midsummer madness. I sneaked a final glance along the length of the carriage and a quick peek into the two either side to check I really was hidden from view. I couldn't see a soul.

That summer's day I'd been wearing a white halterneck dress of light cotton: with trembling hands I gathered the skirt up towards me, exposing first my knees, then my thighs and then a tiny triangle of pink cotton, my panties, which I noticed were already spotted with my own juices. All the while, the rhythm of the train rocked my body: its sure, steady tempo delivered a regular, reliable stimulation. The breeze blowing through the carriage caused my dress to ripple along my body, fluttering across my breasts: I could see my own reflection in detail under the train's harsh striplighting and could clearly make out my pink cheeks, flushed with heat and arousal and two big, hard nipples straining against my bra. I walked my fingers down to the lace trim of my panties and slid my index finger between the cotton and my skin, feeling for my clit. The tip of my finger found the quivering bud and I let out a moan of pleasure that turned within seconds to one of frustration as the train's rhythm slowed and it ground to a halt. As the next station approached, I pulled my hand out of my underwear and crossed my legs again, praying that no one embark on this carriage and spoil my fun.

But at the next station, the doors slid open and a lone man entered. Damn, I thought, so physically frustrated that I felt hot tears prick behind my eyelids. So that's my little masturbation scene over. The stranger who had so rudely interrupted my reverie chose a seat on the same side of the carriage as me, only a couple of metres away: not close enough to be threatening, but close enough for me to check him out. The smell of his aftershave wafted through the carriage. I recognised the scent: a heady, musky cologne I've always liked, a classic designer fragrance, but it's always smelled like sex to me. The guy was tall — at least six foot four — and well built, with shaggy dark-blond hair sunbleached to pale gold around his temples. He couldn't have been more than twenty-five, but his forehead was craggy with one line that ran down the middle. He also had blue eyes and a Brad Pitt pout, sweet, vulnerable features on an otherwise rugged face. Beads of sweat stayed on his unshaven upper lip and his white T-shirt was damp with perspiration. He sprawled in his seat, lean legs spread wide in crisp navy denim, new white-and-red trainers on his feet. Big feet, I noticed, and wondered automatically if the rest of him was in proportion.

I bit my lip, diverted my thoughts to the report I had to write in the morning, tried to study the adverts on the tube, hoping that concentrating on commercials for head lice and car insurance would dampen down the fire of lust that I'd kindled between my legs. I'd assumed the presence of a complete stranger would be enough to snap me out of my little fantasy and bring me back to my senses. But if anything, he made me feel hornier: to be so close to a man and not be able to have him was far worse than having no man around at all.

We pulled out of the station and as the train was swallowed up by the Tube tunnel, I checked myself out in the window again. My skin was still flushed, and my nipples erect and — oh, my God — I realised that although I'd removed my hand from my panties, I hadn't pulled my skirt down properly. My thighs and the gusset of my underwear were on display for him to see. I glanced at his reflection in the mirror, trying subtly to guage whether he had seen me in my exposed and aroused state.

Oh, he was looking all right, though he snatched his eyes away the second he saw me studying his reflection. And he'd obviously liked what he'd seen: his long legs shifted awkwardly as he tried to conceal the beginnings of a hard-on. The thought of his cock made me catch my breath and as I gasped, he looked directly at me for a second. I whipped my head around to face him but before I could make eye contact with him he looked away, cheeks blazing, trying even harder to hide his erection. But it was now too big to hide: I could tell from the bulge inbetween his legs that his dick was tall and broad just as he was.

And the thought of it just flipped a switch somewhere inside me: this is where I went crazy. I closed my eyes, knowing that he would be watching, and spread my legs. I slid my hand down between them and rubbed my index finger over my gusset, gently stroking my clit through my cotton knickers. Up and down, up and down, my finger went, keeping time to the rise and fall of the train's rhythm. The movement of my hand was soft and subtle, but the effect it had on me was far from it: I could feel my pussy swell and moisten, prepare itself for whatever happened next.

I heard the unmistakeable sound of a zipper fly being pulled down. I guessed if he was getting his dick out, it was okay to look. I opened my eyes, turned to see him pull down the waistband of his briefs and out popped a beautiful pink cock. He stroked it in time with the train, in time with me, teasing the purple tip of his penis out from under his foreskin until a hard, thick erection was proudly sticking out from his crotch while his balls remained bulging inside his jeans.

I looked at his cock, my eyes wide, mouth slightly open. Then I looked at his face. We smiled shyly at each other: he watched as I pulled my panties to one side and started touching my clit directly, circular, massaging strokes that I was expert in – sometimes, I'm my favourite lover. But I was transfixed on him as his left hand made smooth, firm strokes up and down his twitching penis, keeping the same rhythm as me, up and down, up and down. My whole body tingled from the intense throbbing in my pussy and clit. Pins and needles tortured my limbs, turning me to jelly. I was so near to having the most powerful orgasm of my life.

But fate – or Transport for London – intervened before I could come, as the train shuddered to an unexpected halt. It always stops at exactly this point on the track – something to do with signals – but my travelling companion obviously didn't take this line very often, because he looked surprised. The timing couldn't have been better: if the jolt of the carriage hadn't interrupted him, I could tell by the frenzied way he was tugging at his dick and the glazed expression in his eyes that thirty seconds more and he'd have come there and then.

That realisation empowered and emboldened me: the thought of him ejaculating in front of me, because of me, was a turn on. But I also knew that I didn't want that erection going to waste. I wanted to get right on in there. He was trembling in his seat, frozen to the spot by desire.

So I moved towards him. I tore my hands away from my throbbing clit and let my dress fall down, covering my panties. Apart from my flushed face and my protruding nipples, I looked the picture of innocence. As I made my unsteady way towards him, each step forced my engorged pussy lips to rub together, increasing the stimulation, making me cry out in delicious pain. It was the sweetest agony I had ever felt.

Close up, I could smell fresh sweat mixed with his aftershave, a raw, horny smell that turned my desire up a level – from mere agony to absolutely unbearable. We looked at each other for a few seconds, half-smiling, half-deadly serious. Someone started speaking in a breathless gravelly voice. I realised it was me.

'I don't make a habit of approaching strangers,' I heard myself saying. 'But it's like this. I want you – no, I *need* you inside me. I happen to know that the train will stay like this for about a minute and a half. I've got to have you – now.'

'Well then,' he said, that sexy, shy grin lighting up his rugged face, 'We'd better not waste any more time.' And he pulled me over by the hem of my skirt, hands feeling for my cotton thong and then swiftly pulling it down. He rested one finger on my clitoris and then slid it into my pussy. Withdrawing his hand, he held it to his nose and with eyes closed, inhaled. 'You're ready for me,' he said, his voice breaking. 'You're *so* ready.'

In reply, I parted my legs so they were either side of his lap and pulled up my skirt for him to have a good look at my pussy: I didn't want him to miss a thing. I lowered myself on to the trembling tip of his dick, letting the rounded end rest against my pussy lips for a few seconds until neither of us could bear it any longer. Which was all of two seconds. I lowered myself down, letting his thick, sturdy cock prise apart my slit and open me, penetrate me and finally fill me up and give me what I needed so badly. I pounded my pussy on to his dick, pushing down with my whole bodyweight, swallowing him up. I wanted to recapture the first thrill of penetration again, so I raised myself up on my thighs until his cock was nearly out of me, then I sunk down again, hard. My knees grazed the rough carpet of the train seats but I didn't feel it then. Every time I sank down on to his hard-on it seemed bigger: I felt fuller, more satisfied, nearer to my orgasm.

I had one hand on his shoulder to steady myself, the other hand on the window leaving sweaty fingerprints on the glass. I caught my reflection: a woman I barely recognised, riding a total stranger as he rode the train.

His hands squeezed and slapped my arse, guiding my hips up and down on his dick. My tits were level with his face. There wasn't time for him to untie my dress and free them so he licked and bit at my nipples through the thin cotton, with a greedy, almost vicious mouth. I needed him to bite me hard so that the sensations in my tits could compete with the intensity of what went on down below.

'I'm gonna come,' he said, face twisted. 'I'm gonna come inside you,'

'I want you to,' I whispered breathlessly back, 'But hold back for one second. It'll be so good, I promise you.'

He clenched his eyes and tensed his whole body, trying to control his orgasm. But he was losing the battle.

'I can't . . .' he whimpered. 'I'm coming . . . oh God, I'm coming so hard . . .'

Just in time, the train roared into life with a judder that we both felt. It was what I had been waiting for: the convulsion of the engine sent a shiver down the length of the carriage and the seat beneath us lurched. The delicious vibrations travelled up through his feet, his cock, up to my clit and triggered my climax: I came around his hard-on, my pussy squeezing and releasing his dick, sucking the life out of it, making me weak as I abandoned my body to the orgasm. I shuddered as the waves of pleasure subsided, buried my head in his chest, my sweat mingling with his as we both began to recover.

There was no time to waste holding each other: the driver announced that we were about to arrive at the next stop – my home station. I eased myself off him, relishing the final sensation as his dick emerged from my sore, sensitive but satisfied pussy. I stepped out of my panties, already soaking with my juices, and used them to wipe away the spunk that trickled out of me. Knowing I'd never see this man again, I tossed them on to his lap – a parting gift.

I smoothed my hair down and straightened my dress.

By the time the doors sighed open at the deserted platform, I looked like just another girl on another day, one of a million Tube journeys taken by a million workers.

I left him there on the Tube, his dick still slowly going down, a little trickle of cum leaking on to his jeans. He was laughing to himself as though he couldn't believe what he'd just done. If I couldn't still smell him on me, I would have felt the same. At least my love affair with the Underground had been reignited.

I don't think I'll ever see him again – he didn't look like a regular commuter. But that doesn't stop me looking for a face in the crowds during rush hour or the sudden flood of arousal that takes me over whenever I find myself standing next to a male passenger wearing a certain cologne.

DIGITS

Who says you have to be in the same room as someone to have great sex with them?

The phone rang at 3.30 a.m. I knew it was him. Who else would call me at that time? I sat up in bed, suddenly wide awake, satin sheets cascading down my skin, hot and sticky, even though it was a cool night. Had I been dreaming about him? I reached for my mobile, flipped it open, my lips brushed the mouthpiece.

'Talk to me,' I said, without waiting for him to say hello. 'Tell me what to do.'

'Take off your clothes,' he snarled in the deep, masculine voice that was my favourite sound in the world. His tone was gravelly, like the Malboro man, and such an aphrodisiac to me that the actual words he spoke were almost secondary. It was the vocal equivalent of a hand stroking my cunt.

'I'm already naked,' I panted, looking down at my chest. In the moonlight, I could see my breasts swell and

15

rise in anticipation of the sex talk ahead. 'I knew you'd call. Don't ask me how, but I knew. I was waiting for you. I wanted to be ready.'

'Go hands-free. You'll need to tonight,' he said, and I felt my clitoris begin to tingle. I fumbled in my bedside drawer for the mobile headset, hooked it over my ear, lay back on my pillows and awaited further instructions.

'Lick your fingers, one by one,' said the voice in the darkness. I did so, making sure that I made a little kiss-like noise as each finger left my lips. Ten times. On his end of the line, I heard, with a thrill, the noise of a belt buckle loosening, a fly being undone. I imagined his cock, far away – but controlled by the thought of me, growing with the sound of my voice, stiffening at the thought of my body responding to its owner's instructions. It was empowering and wildly arousing, and the first droplets of moisture seeped from me, made a tiny damp patch on the bedsheets.

'Now make circles on your tits. *Around* your nipples, don't touch them.' I did as he asked, delighted by the way my nipples hardened at my teasing caress.

'Tell me how it feels. What's happening to you?'

'It feels good,' I said. 'My nipples are stiff as fuck. Hard and pink, like two strawberries. I've never seen them this big. But I need to touch them so much I can't bear it. I can't fucking stand it!'

'Lick your finger again and pinch your right nip.

Imagine it's me sucking on that tit, like a baby. Pinch it hard: the harder you grip it, the harder my dick gets.'

I responded, and the relief was sweet for a few seconds before the sharp pain made me cry out. 'Oh, that's too much!' I cried down the phone. 'I can't take it! It feels too good.'

'Sit on your right hand,' he said. 'I want you to squash that hand till it's numb.'

Well, that was a new request, and a little quirky, and it briefly interrupted my arousal, but what the hell – I had to trust him. I slid my right hand under my butt and let the weight of my body press down on it. Although he hadn't instructed me to, I turned the pleasure up a notch by inserting the knuckle of my thumb between my arse cheeks, making a little buttplug that I could feel sliding up and down that secret, sensitive area whenever I moved. His breathing was audible on the other end of the line: it was as arousing as though I could feel the heat of his breath on my neck.

'With your left hand, trail your fingers up and down your body, over your tits, your belly. Keep it light as a feather.'

'Oh, that tickles!' I breathed into my headset. 'You're making me shiver.'

'Can you reach your bedside drawer without taking your right hand away?' he asked.

'Yeah,' I said, getting excited – opening the bedside drawer could only mean one thing.

'Reach inside and take out your Rabbit,' he said. My free hand found the Rabbit in no time. It was a beautiful sex-toy – a hot-pink, top-of-the-range vibrator with little whirring bunny ears to stimulate the skin either side of my clitoris, and a big, thick shaft, the size and shape of the world's most perfect dick, filled with tiny rolling pearls that rotated inside me, caressing me inside and out.

'Turn it on and hold it up to the phone. I want to hear it,' he said, 'cos then I can picture it inside you.' I set the balls whirring and held the Rabbit up to the phone.

'Oh, yeah,' he said. 'That sounds good. Really good. Now it's on, I want you to slide it in you. Are you wet enough?' He spat, to lube up his own dick as he played with it. I imagined his hard-on, as solid and big as the toy I was looking at and growing by the second.

'I'm so wet,' I told him, and it was the truth. His voice always triggers my juices, but coupled with the Rabbit, I was really soaking. Even the *sight* of my Rabbit has me creaming like nothing else, because I know there's a guaranteed climax when it comes out to play.

'Put it inside you,' he said. 'Do it slow. I want to hear it.'

I parted my legs, and inch by inch, I penetrated myself with the vibrating dildo. 'It's going in now,' I breathed.

'It's just making its way past my pussy lips. It's halfway in, it's disappearing. It's in! It's all the way in! I'm fucking myself with it now.'

As I thrust the toy deep into my cunt, my body muffled the buzzing sound: I knew that he loved to hear the toy buzz as I drew it in and out of my hole, so I gave him the aural treat he was after. I pulled the Rabbit in and out, in and out, letting it whirr loud and soft, loud and soft. His grunts on the other end of the line told me my party trick had hit the spot. As the toy whirled and swirled inside me, I could feel my pussy walls start to spasm in anticipation of the climax and the front of my cunt, right by my G-spot felt warm and heightened.

'Keep it still,' he said. 'Now, turn on the clit stim, but keep it on the lowest setting.' I loved the way his orders were so specific: it was as though he was caressing me, inch by inch, plotting the co-ordinates on my body that reacted most strongly, mapping out my erogenous zones with his words. I flipped another switch, and the little bunny ears began softly to hum, soft rubber caresses, on either side of my clit. The effect was instant and electric, sending shockwaves of pleasure throughout my whole body. In the time it took to inhale and exhale loudly so he could hear, my pussy and clit had become the centre of the universe. I concentrated all the energy I possessed in this area so when that ball of power was released, my climax would overwhelm me. I had to be careful: once these little knobs of rubber kicked in, I could come within seconds.

'I'm warning you, I'm close to coming,' I said. 'I'm really close. Is your dick hard? Because I want you to come right when I do.'

'Hang on in there. I've got one more instruction for you,' he said, between gasps. I could hear a slapping noise coming from the receiver: his hand working his dick, the rhythm growing faster and faster. 'Now take that hand out from under you,' he said. 'Is it numb?' It was: completely dead. I couldn't feel a thing. I told him as much.

'Good,' he said, his voice wavering, as if he was having trouble getting the words out. 'Okay, take that right hand and play with your tits again. Imagine it's *my* hand. Shut your eyes – it's not you touching yourself. It's me, feeling you, stroking *you*.'

I dragged the unfeeling hand across my chest. Because it was numb it really did feel as if it were a lover's touch, someone else's hand, nothing to do with me. This sensation blurred fantasy and reality, and for one lust-fuelled, crazy moment I wondered if he was actually in the room with me. But the deep breathing in my earpiece reminded me that I was only having phone sex. I awaited his final instruction.

'Okay,' he said. 'Turn everything up as far as it will

go.' With my left hand, I flipped the switches that would intensify the buzzing on the clit stim and send the pearls inside me whirling at warp speed, massaging my insides, caressing my G-spot. Within a few seconds, the hot waves of orgasm washed over me. I forgot about everything but the grunting in my ear and the feelings in my pussy and clit: my lips went slack and my eyes glazed over: the room around me swum in and out of focus.

'Tell me how it feels,' he said, loud, insistent. I could barely form the words.

'So good . . . so good . . . ooooooooooooooooh,' I just about managed.

It was a long, strong orgasm that lasted a good ten seconds: one, two, three, four, five, six overwhelming spasms that rocked my body and made me cry out, a wordless wail of ecstasy, into the headset. I whipped out the Rabbit, unable to take any more stimulation. My pussy was swollen, dark red, utterly satisfied.

I stayed on the phone, urging him on to his own orgasm. I could tell by his repeated cries of, 'Oh yeah . . . oh yeah . . .' that he wasn't far behind me. Then the six seconds' silence that always preceded his orgasm. I loved that moment, frozen in time: I pictured his face as he tipped over the edge and climaxed, balls finally relieved of all the spunk, letting it shoot out in a hot, white jet across the room, while I thought, 'I made that happen.'

Then a final 'Oh *yeah*,' as he came, this time in a deep growl that made me shiver all over. I waited another few seconds for him to come back down to earth.

'Please,' he said, his voice back to its normal tone, no longer my sex god but just another man on the end of the line. 'Please, who are you? When can we meet?'

I didn't answer. I hung up, like I always do. Once I've come and he's come, what's the point in making small talk? It's not like he's here: why waste time on post-coital pleasantries?

I lay back between the sheets, although I knew it would be hours before my heart rate returned to normal and I was able to sleep. My mind was racing, thinking back to that evening six months ago when a guy had called the wrong number and had got me and something about his voice had made me keep him on the line, start a little flirty talk.

You see, I'm having the best sex of my life with this guy. It'd be such a shame to risk spoiling all that by meeting him.

THE MAGIC TOYSHOP

I've always believed that sex shops have a magical quality to them: stepping through the door is like walking into another world, where possibilities you'd never dreamed of are suddenly a reality. It's like an adult version of finding Narnia at the back of the wardrobe, or the Secret Garden behind the wall. A very, very adult version!

Even the shyest customers can find that the atmosphere in these erotic boutiques unleashes a certain lack of inhibition . . . the woman in this story found that her life changed for ever when she set foot in a sex shop for the very first time.

I was twenty-seven years of age before I went into a sex shop. Does that seem old to you? It did to me: my friends were always telling me about this vibrator, that strap-on, blindfolds, paddles, dildos and a whole pleasure chest of other playthings they used to spice up their sex lives. When they expressed their opinions on the latest hi-tech vibrator or a hot new DVD, I'd nod and giggle with the rest of them, but I barely knew what they were talking about. The truth was, I was just never that confident when it came to sex: when it came to sex shopping, I didn't really know where to start. How could I decide what kind of toy to buy? Friends said you just asked the people who worked in the sex shop, but that was out of the question for a shy girl like me. I blush and get tongue-tied taking a jumper back to Marks and Spencer: there's no way I could have asked some cool, knowing girl behind the counter of a sex shop which toy was most likely to bring me to orgasm.

Because that was my other secret. I'd never had an orgasm. Well, actually, I wasn't sure: everyone says if you've had one you know about it, but I was uncertain of quite what to make of the warm, fizzy feelings I'd get when I touched myself in bed at night, or when I was fooling around with boyfriends. I'd experienced sensations that seemed promising and frustrating, but were nothing like the fireworks and orchestras you read about. In my women's glossies I'd gathered that a vibrator would be a fairly guaranteed route to said fireworks, so I resolved to buy one and finally discover what all the fuss was about. But whenever I passed an adult shop, I'd make excuses to myself: I was too busy, too tired. Somehow I just never got round to it.

That all changed one Saturday afternoon last April. I was out shopping when I noticed a little store tucked away in the basement of a Georgian townhouse. A pink-and-silver sign told me the shop was called 'Miss Kiss'. Discreet and feminine, there were curvy mannequins in the window decked out in fabulous lingerie and brandishing diamond-studded leather whips. Clearly this was a shop that sold more than pretty knickers and bras. Force of habit made me turn on my heel and walk away, but when I looked back over my shoulder, the pink beaded curtain appeared so welcoming and female-friendly that I thought, what the hell, it's now or never, I might as well go for it. My feet carried me down the cast-iron staircase before my head had time to talk me out of it.

Once there, I pushed back the curtain and entered another world. On the left hand side of the shop were racks and racks of exquisite lingerie, not the tacky, scratchy stuff I'd have expected, but chiffon and ribbons and pastel colours as well as more dramatic black-and-red burlesque garments. To the right were the books and films. Through an archway into a different section at the back, was where a comprehensive selection of toys were. A large chrome dildo was lit up like a sculpture in the end. I wasn't the only customer: normal women, like me, were calmly walking around the shop as though it were a supermarket, picking up graphic sex books, browsing explicit porno-graphic DVDs. Apart from the girl on the till who smiled a friendly hello, no one looked twice at me. Certainly no one seemed to think it was strange that someone like me was in a place like this.

I didn't know where to start, so I gravitated towards the lingerie, the only part of the shop I didn't feel out of my depth in. I picked up a couple of items I particularly liked the look of: a pastel-pink chiffon babydoll minidress and a corset made of shimmering turquoise silk. Not the kind of things I'd wear in a million years, but I felt better now that I was carrying something. More like a real customer.

I looked at the shelves of movies and magazines, felt bombarded with images of women who had clearly had orgasms before, probably had them regularly; so many bodies, so many combinations, so many images. It was thrilling, but a little intimidating.

Next, I spent a few minutes in the little cavern of a room where the sex toys were housed. It was like an Aladdin's den of pure pleasure. There were brightly coloured glittery dildos made of plastic; lifelike, flesh-coloured ones that were so huge I blushed for all the boyfriends I'd ever had; chrome sticks; silver shafts; dildos with two ends; fake penises made of leather; some knobbled, like corn; some with batteries, some without, and, I swear, some with reams of cable that plugged into the mains. I should have been like a kid in a candy store, but I felt a mounting sense of panic and confusion.

'Can I help you?' came a voice from behind me. It

was the girl behind the counter. About my age, she was as pretty as a pixie with short hair dyed pillarbox-red. She looked like she'd never known a day's inhibition her whole life, and although she was friendly, I didn't feel able to approach her. So I did what I've always done in these situations. I chickened out.

'I'm, er, I'd just like to try these on,' I said, gesturing towards the clothes in my arms.

'Cool,' said the salesgirl. 'The fitting room is just up those stairs.' She pointed to a tiny doorway at the back of the shop. I went through another beaded curtain and up a staircase lit with strings of fairylights. At the top I found two tiny but opulent dressing rooms: padded satin doors hid red plush benches and full-length gilt mirrors.

Glad to be alone, I took off my clothes and tried on the babydoll dress. I examined myself from every angle. It was flattering, I'd admit that: the built-in bra pushed up my small breasts, making them look high, round and full, while the marabou-trimmed skirt skimmed my arse, making my legs look long and lean. But I looked cutesy and I'd had enough of looking cute. I was here to tap into my inner sex goddess, not my inner Baby Spice.

I hung the pretty garment back on its padded hanger and picked up the turquoise corset. It was more like a work of art than an item of clothing, embroidered with intricate chinoiserie patterns, tiny dragons and flames chasing each other across the silk. Depending on which way the light caught it, the material could be blue, or emerald or even gold. I held it up against me: the colour made my green eyes shine out. The corset fastened with a black silk cord which threaded through a series of eyelets and tied up at the top: well, that was the idea. Holding it in the air, I couldn't even work out which way up it was supposed to go. As I got tangled in the black laces, I felt increasingly silly and frustrated.

'Need a hand with that?' came a female voice from outside my cubicle door. 'I can help you get into it.' I panicked: I was naked inside the changing room. Naked, hot and flustered. But I tried to be calm and mature: what the hell, I thought, she works here, she's probably seen worse people than me naked, she probably sees dozens of pairs of tits every day. Holding this thought and feigning a casualness I didn't really feel, I let her in.

This salesgirl was a tiny Nordic-looking woman with pale blue eyes and white-blonde hair in a long braid coiled around her head. She wore what I thought of as sex-shop worker or fetish clothes: a black corset, clumpy platform boots in black leather with silver panels on the toes, fishnet stockings and a short tartan miniskirt. But her face was free of make-up, making her look sweet and vulnerable despite her aggressive outfit.

'I'm Alice,' she said briskly, as though this were any changing room in a normal high-street shop, and I wasn't naked, or about to be laced into a corset by a complete stranger. 'Let me give you a hand.' Although her English was perfect, she had a faint accent that I couldn't place. Perhaps she was Swedish.

With a breezy confidence, she turned me around so that I was looking at myself in the mirror. 'Arms up!' she said. I obeyed, raising them above my head, feeling very exposed, and confused because this wasn't an unpleasant feeling, not at all . . . as Alice held the corset against my body, she drew her arms around me so that they encircled my waist.

'Where you're going wrong,' she said, as she threaded the black laces behind me with deft, tiny fingers, 'Is thinking this is a *normal* corset.' As she spoke, I felt the bones of the corset constrict around me, cupping my waist, squeezing my flesh. 'Your breasts are actually supposed to sit *on top* of the corset, so your nipples are exposed. Like this,' she said, and before I could stop her she had lifted up first my left breast, and then my right, so that they perched just on top of the corset. Alice's touch, which had started off brisk and businesslike, grew tender as she arranged each breast into its cup, handling my nipples as tenderly as a lover would, making sure they were just visible over the top of the corset. The poked over the top of the stiff, boned silk, so pale and pink they would have been invisible – except that, to my shame, I felt them growing hard under Alice's small, soft fingers.

'You have exceptionally beautiful breasts,' she said. Even in my limited experience of sex shops, I was aware that lavish compliments like this were unusual. But I wanted her to go on: as she described my body it seemed to come alive, and tremble. I wanted her to talk about each part of me, to wake up every inch of my skin by describing it in that funny, sing-song voice she had.

'And that colour is fabulous on you. Makes your skin look like milk, and really brings out the colour of your eyes.' Alice's own eyes lit up. 'I've got just the thing that would go with that!' And before I could say another thing, she disappeared from the cubicle and scurried down the stairs.

Alone again, I admired myself in the mirror. I had to admit that Alice was right: I looked hot! I wasn't used to seeing myself as so overtly sexy, and it was unleashing a confidence I didn't know I possessed. My breasts looked magnificent, and my waist – never normally my best feature – appeared tiny, cinched in by the corset. I struck a pose, squeezed my arms together to push up my breasts and, growing bolder, I parted my legs and bent over to show my arse off. As I looked at my skinny white butt, I wondered if Alice would like it. Although no one was touching me, the tingling feelings that I'd thought might be an orgasm were starting to ripple through my body again, but this time, they were more intense than ever, and I somehow knew that this wasn't an orgasm, but might be the first step on the road to one.

I don't know how long Alice had been watching me posing in the mirror, but when I looked round she was there, big blue eyes wide and unblinking, her lips parted and slightly moist. She held some slips of silk and a carrier bag emblazoned with the Miss Kiss logo in her arms.

'Don't stop,' whispered Alice, her voice turning husky. 'You look mesmerising.'

'No, really, I was just messing about, it's just that . . .' I began to protest, but Alice was in the changing room, tipping her bag on to the floor and closing the door behind her before I could finish my sentence.

'Try these on,' she said, and handed me a pair of tiny panties in the same iridescent silk as the corset, tied at the sides with the same black lace.

'Let me,' she said, bending down and holding out the panties for me to step into. Her face was level with my pussy. Her warm breath caressed me there, like the ghost of a kiss, and it lit the touchpaper for a tiny, intense fire that began to burn between my legs. Although I'd never felt anything like this excited before, there was no mistaking what it was – lust: powerful, irresistible, overwhelming

31

lust. Could Alice feel the heat I was radiating? Would she know how aroused I was?

If she did, she was doing her best to get me ever hornier. She slid the lingerie up my legs, her hands travelling along my shins, then the front of my thighs, before arranging the panties neatly on my pelvis. Again, her touch was tender, lingering, as though she took as much pleasure in touching me as I did from feeling her hands on my skin. Alice stood to face me, hands travelling up to my waist, smoothing the fabric of my corset, fingers flying over my nipples with a featherlight touch. Our faces were inches away from each other: did she read the same desire in me that I saw in her?

'Look at you. You're beautiful,' she said, turning to face the mirror.

Wow! I'd never seen myself look so good, but it was something more than just sexy underwear. It was an unfamiliar blush, lips that looked darker and larger than normal, breasts that rose and fell more dramatically than usual, and a look in my eyes that was brand new to me. Alice was behind me now, looking over my shoulder. She went back to salesgirl mode, untying the corset and then lacing it tighter.

'In the past, this would have been tied so tight that you couldn't breathe. It's about exaggerating the most dramatic parts of the female form, which is beautiful anyway: well, yours is,' she said, her eyes sweeping up and down the length of my body. 'You see, the corset shapes your waist, and scoops up your tits,' she said, her hands hovering over the relevant body parts as she spoke. The hand that fluttered around my breast froze in mid-air and then, slowly and deliberately, Alice placed her cupped hand over my breast and did . . . nothing. Absolutely nothing. She didn't need to. The heat and energy of her touch and the electric current that seemed to pass between us was enough. My nipple became harder than I ever thought it could, standing to attention like an unscrewed lipstick, poking through Alice's fingers. And still she stayed there, motionless, as fascinated as I was by the way my body responded to her. I'm sure that if we had stayed still together like that, I'd have come just from the touch of her hand.

But we didn't stay still: whatever was exploding inside me had other ideas, and I turned around to face Alice. Although she was tiny, in her platform boots she was exactly my height. When I leaned in to press my lips to hers, it felt soft and natural. Although I'd never kissed another girl before, I felt more alive and confident than I ever had with men. She parted her lips and let me dart my tongue in and out of her mouth. She kissed back so softly it was almost imperceptible. Worried that I had gone too far, I drew away.

'I'm sorry,' I said, 'I couldn't help it. I've never done this before. I don't want to get you into trouble, but you make me feel . . .'

'I wanted you to,' Alice said, bowing her head to look at my breasts, eyelashes tickling my cheeks. 'I don't want you to stop. In fact, now that we've started, I can't leave you alone.'

Alice pulled at my panties, undoing the bows that she had tied just seconds earlier. They fell around my ankles. Her hands rested on my buttocks for a moment and then she parted my arse cheeks, slid one hand between my legs from behind and one in front: she clasped her hands together, creating a cradle for my pussy where the panties had been. Her hands were soft and warm as she held them there, I felt wetness flood my slit and ooze on to her.

'You're wet,' she said, unclasping her fingers and gently pulling my pussy lips apart.

I didn't have the words to tell Alice how good that felt, so I communicated my desire to her with a long, soft kiss: my tongue probed her mouth, I took her full lower lip between my teeth and sucked it, and she swirled her tongue around my lips. Her nimble fingers found my clitoris: she made a V with her two forefingers, placing one on either side of the swollen bud and stroked gently. The effect was immediate: the dampness between my legs became a trickle as my body's reflexes tried to keep up with the pleasure she was administering to it. Alice leaned heavily into me, forcing my back up against the gilt mirror. The glass was icy cold on my back, another sensation for my poor, confused, yet desperately horny body to cope with. I cried out in shock. She placed a finger to my lips, shushing me in case other customers heard us: I could smell myself on her hands.

We kissed again, my tits crushed against Alice. I could feel her nipples through the mesh of her top, as hard as mine. As I slid my hands up her top my fingers were shaking. The feel of another woman's breast beneath my fingers was new to me, and Alice's tits were small, warm, her nipples hot and hard. Her firm, young flesh yielded to my touch then sprang back when I took my fingers away. The harder I kneaded her tits, the faster she caressed my clit. When she withdrew I moaned, grabbed her wrist, tried to force her hand back between my legs again because I didn't want the pleasure to stop – not now, not when I could feel my body getting closer and closer to something beautiful.

'Don't worry. You'll like this,' said Alice, an impish smile on her face. 'I'm going to taste you,' and with that she dropped to her knees. She parted my trembling legs and swirled her tongue around my inner thighs. She was teasing me, taunting me, before finally diving into the pleasure zone, her tongue as lively as a little fish darting all over my clitoris so quickly I could barely register one thrilling sensation before the next.

I was so horny I didn't think I could stand it. I felt the first vague pulse, like a bass drum being played in the next house, becoming louder and faster with every beat of my heart. I reached for my own breasts, groping them, massaging them, remembering how Alice's small budding tits had felt under my fingers, closing my eyes, pretending they were hers.

Suddenly she stopped.

'No! *Don't!*' I begged. 'You can't stop now! Please . . . I'm getting so close . . . I can feel it. Alice . . . you're so good . . . please don't stop.'

'I'm not stopping,' she said, her face glazed with the juices from my pussy. 'I can't stop. You taste too good. I can feel you throbbing in my mouth. I'm not stopping. I'm just making things more interesting.'

Alice reached into her carrier bag and pulled out the sleek chrome dildo I'd seen on the shop floor.

'You'll never come the way you do on your first time with a woman,' Alice said. 'But it's even better if you've got something inside you to come around.'

Without waiting for permission, she thrust the dildo between my legs: it disappeared, sliding effortlessly into my dripping pussy. It was as cold as the mirror had been on the skin of my back and had a strangely pleasurable numbing effect, like pins and needles inside me.

'Now you're ready to come,' she said, and her blonde head resumed its place level with my pussy. I leaned back and sighed as Alice's tongue began working again, the heat my body was generating warmed up the fake dick that she twisted and pumped inside me. The waves of pleasure that had been rising and falling inside my body now crashed together: I knew I was going to come a few seconds before the orgasm hit: my mouth went dry, my vision blurred and then with one final flick of Alice's tongue, the tension I held in my clitoris was released throughout my body, the pleasure spreading up and out like an old-fashioned fan being opened. In movies people say words, whole sentences when they come: I don't know how they can remember what language they speak at a time like that. The noise that came out of me was animal, a long wail of pleasure and relief as my pussy jerked and twitched and clutched at the dildo.

Okay. I think I can now officially say I know what an orgasm feels like, I thought.

Alice watched me as I recovered from the experience, pulled the dildo out of my pussy and licked the length of it.

'I'm gonna come so fast,' she said, clicking her fingers to indicate how long she would need to reach her own orgasm. 'You've got me so worked up I'm throbbing. But I need a little help.'

She pulled her top over her head exposing her breasts. They looked like they felt, peaches-and-cream tits that were firm with slightly pointed nipples. I fell on them, sucked them hard: I could fit a whole tit in my mouth and I felt her nipple tickle the roof of my mouth as my tongue explored the fleshy underside of her breast. She was using the tip of the chrome dildo to massage her own clitoris, her hand fluttering as fast as a hummingbird's wings.

'Oooooh,' she breathed, as her body trembled and her nipples quivered between my lips. 'Ooooh, that's good. So good.'

It took a few seconds for Alice to compose herself, and then she flipped back into salesgirl mode. 'I think you should get this corset,' she said, undoing my back and shaking out the laces before handing me the garment. She kissed me on the lips and opened the changing room door.

'I'll see you downstairs,' she said, and then with a wink, 'Not a word about this to anyone.' She replaced the dildo in its bag and backed out of the room, one finger on her pursed lips. I left the babydoll dress on its hanger but there was no way I was leaving without buying the silk underwear set. Every time I looked at the fabric – fuck, every time I saw something in that shimmering turquoise-gold colour – it would be enough to trigger powerful memories of what had just happened.

I changed back into my clothes and went downstairs to the shop. I looked in every corner of it for Alice, but she was nowhere to be seen. Puzzled, I took the corset and panties to the red-haired salesgirl who was still behind the counter. Did she know I'd just fucked her colleague? If she did, she wasn't saying anything.

'Good choice,' she said, as she wrapped my purchases in tissue paper.

'Thanks,' I said automatically, and then summoned up the courage to ask where Alice was. 'I said I'd meet her down here, you see,' I said, by way of explanation. 'Is she working out the back, or something?'

'Who?' The red-haired girl looked puzzled. 'I'm the only person working here today,' she said. 'We don't have any staff on the shop floor or in the changing rooms.'

'Then who was . . . ?' I began, but let it go. I wandered out into the street, my mind racing.

I still don't know who Alice was, or how she came to be in that changing room.

Maybe she's just an opportunist who likes to hang around sex shops hoping for naïve young women to seduce. And to be honest, I don't really care. Because I might have gone into that shop a naïve young woman, but I came out feeling empowered, confident, more sure of my sexuality and knowing exactly what miracles my body is capable of. In fact, it's time I passed on the lesson to someone else. Perhaps it's time I went back to Miss Kiss and hung around in the changing rooms looking for a nervous young customer to assist . . .

BUCKLE MY SHOE

I have two great passions in life. Shoe shopping and sex. This lucky woman got to combine the two . . . I'm still searching for this guy myself!

Most first dates tend to take place after dark: dinner, drinks, maybe a club. But my first date with Nick got off to a much earlier start. He told me to meet him at Bond Street tube station at 11 a.m. on a Saturday. It was my first clue that Nick was a little . . . different.

I'd met Nick a couple of weeks before at a friend's birthday party. It was a fancy dress thing: I'd gone as a Roman centurion, accessorising a toga minidress with a pair of gold sandals with bronzed leather laces which bound my legs, criss-crossing all the way up to the knee. Friends passed comment that my outfit had a certain kinky kind of appeal but Nick's reaction when he saw me proved it. He looked me up, then down, and his eyes stayed on my sandals, staring at my feet with such intensity I was relieved I'd taken the time to have a deluxe pedicure that afternoon. I was used to men who checked out my tits when they spoke to me, but to be upstaged by my feet? That was a whole new experience.

I liked Nick right away. He was funny, smart and well dressed – he'd come as a gangster, but in an Armani suit. Nice touch. I liked his voice, too: educated and classy. And he looked great: light brown hair that fell into his eyes and a tall, slim body. We spent all night chatting, and when he'd asked for my number at the end of the night, I was happy to oblige. The kiss he gave me by the door before seeing me into a cab confirmed I'd done the right thing. Lingering, sensitive but firm too, it promised great things. I was looking forward to our date.

And now here he was at the Tube station, dressed-to-kill in a soft, grey cashmere jumper and D&G jeans. I was dressed for the daytime in low-slung jeans, a pair of flats and a vest top. Nick said hello with another one of those soft kisses, full of possibility, then took my arm and steered me away from Oxford Street and towards the posh boutiques and department stores of Bond Street, the ones I usually walk past because I can't afford to shop there.

'I'd like to take you shopping,' he said, in his public schoolboy accent. 'Is that all right with you?'

'Very much so,' I said, thrilled at the thought of giving Nick's credit card a workout in London's finest shops. We walked past Cartier, Tiffany and Gucci, then came to a stop outside a chic little shoe shop. The window was full of exquisite jewelled sandals and Italian leather stilettos.

'We need to get you out of those awful flat shoes,' he said. I looked down at the shabby ballet pumps on my feet: not the sexiest shoes in the world, but they were comfortable and I loved them.

'I remember what pretty feet and legs you have,' said Nick, softening his insult. 'It's the first thing I noticed about you. It's a sin to hide them away in shoes like that when you should be showing them off to the world. Well, to me at least,' his eyes twinkling as he flashed a mischievous grin and dragged me over the threshold into the shop.

While I sat on a banquette in the middle of the store, Nick prowled around the shelves, selecting the shoes he wanted me to try on: pretty sales assistants fawned over him as though he were a regular big spender here. I thought Nick's insistence on choosing the shoes a little odd, but charming: since he was paying, he may as well select the goodies.

Ready for my Cinderella moment, I slipped off my pumps and wiggled my toes. To my shock, Nick lifted my foot on to his lap and caressed it. His hands were smooth and expensively manicured. With his thumb, he pressed down on the inside of my ankle, tiny massaging actions sending a pleasurable frisson up my spine. 'In reflexology,' he said, in a voice so low I had to lean in close to hear it, 'this part of the foot corresponds directly to the clitoris. If I find the right spot, and apply the right pressure here for long enough, you'll be so aroused you'll be begging for me to touch you there.'

I blushed: I don't know if it was the reflexology or just being so close to such a handsome, smart man, but I was beginning to feel a tingle located somewhere altogether more interesting than my ankle. Inside my jeans, I felt the first throb that told me my body was getting ready for sex. That's when Nick inclined his head further towards mine and gave me my second kiss of the day. It was more urgent and probing this time: the pressure of his hand on my foot increased as his tongue forced my lips apart and swirled around my mouth. He slid his forefinger in between two of my toes: no one had ever touched me there before, and the caress was surprisingly intimate and arousing. He then bent down and planted a kiss on my big toe, springing back as the clatter of heels on the wooden floor announced the return of the salesgirls.

They brought us shoeboxes, ten or eleven of them, each box containing a pair Nick wanted me to try. Needless to say, there wasn't a pair of flats among them: all were skyscraper high and in-your-face sexy. I was as excited as a child on Christmas morning.

The first pair of shoes were red 1950s-style Minnie Mouse shoes with bows on the toes. I slipped them on and felt my inner sex kitten stretch and purr. They made me want to walk with a wiggle and pout like a starlet. 'I like you in these,' he said. 'They have kitsch appeal. You can have them if you want, but it's not quite what I'm after. I can't see enough of your feet in them.'

Next up was a pair of black patent sandals with straps little thicker than strands of spaghetti that wound round and round my ankles before tying in a bow: a little bit bondage, a little bit kinky. Once again, my whole body language changed and I found myself taking on the persona of the shoes: I stood before him, thrusting my hips out, playing the confident, don't-fuck-with-me dominatrix. 'Mmmm. That's more like it,' said Nick. 'Trussed up. That's far more sexy.'

He licked his lips, visibly turned on.

As I observed the effect the shoes had on Nick, I grew more confident and aroused. I had a sudden vision of the two of us together: I'd wear nothing but killer heels and I'd make him harder than he'd ever been in his life. He read my mind.

'I'd like to see you on my bed, naked but for those shoes,' he said, the twinkle in his eye replaced by something darker, hungrier, and far more thrilling. 'But try one more pair on for me first.'

He opened a box and took out a pair of diamanté strappy sandals with vertiginous Perspex heels, sharp as ice picks. They were stripper's shoes, call-girl's shoes, shoes for a woman who doesn't have to walk anywhere and always has a man to pay for the taxi. I put my feet in Nick's lap while he fastened the buckles: he helped me on with my left shoe and my right foot felt its way around his lap, looking for his dick. My toes touched on his soft balls then located a growing hard-on. I pressed down with the ball of my foot. Nick closed his eyes and let out a whimper so soft that only I could hear it.

I whipped my foot away, eager to prolong his pleasure, and stood up. The shoes made me stick out my tits and arse, changed my whole posture, made me aware of each curve of my body. I liked the woman I was in them.

'I can't walk in these,' I said, giggling and teetering around on the spiky stilettos. 'I feel dizzy up here.'

'That's the idea. I don't want you to be able to get away.' He was only half-joking.

'Look what you're doing to me,' he said, grabbing my hand and pulling me towards him with such unexpected force that I thought I'd snap an ankle as I stumbled into his arms. 'Look what you and your sexy fucking feet are doing to me,' he repeated, and held my hand to his crotch: I could tell that he was now fully erect. 'If you're as wet as I am hard, I think we should buy these shoes and take them back to my place.' No man had ever taken control of a situation so forcefully before: the words worked like a magic spell and I felt my pussy lips moisten in anticipation.

Nick handed a black Amex card over to the salesgirl who was probably relieved to get these two obviously horny customers out of her shop. 'We'll have this pair,' he said, without even flinching when she rang through £700.

Now the shoes were mine. In them, I was a woman so sexually potent that she could make a man get a hard-on in public and hand over a month's rent in a minute. I was a woman whose own pussy was throbbing along with the soles of her feet. I accepted the shoes with nothing more than a simple 'thank you'. I bent down to take them off, swaying like a baby giraffe as I did so.

'Leave them on,' said Nick to me, and then to the salesgirl, 'Put her old shoes in the box. She's keeping these on.'

We were out of the shop and on Bond Street within seconds. Nick half-dragged, half carried me and extended an arm to hail a taxi. In my new shoes, I was nearly as tall as him. When he pulled me in for a kiss, his dick was level with my pussy. I made a point of pressing the whole of my body into his groin, hinting at what we were going to do together once we got back to his flat.

A cab pulled up alongside us and we drew apart to

clamber in. Nick lay me down on the back seat as gently as though I were a china doll and then sat opposite with my feet cradled in his lap. 'Jesus,' he said, stroking me, 'You make these shoes come alive. I can't wait to see you naked in them.'

Feet had never been an erogenous zone for me before but as Nick took my left foot, pulled it up to his lips and kissed it, I don't think I'd ever felt so highly charged. I surrendered to the extraordinary intimacy of letting a man's mouth work its magic on this secret, hidden part of my body. I watched my pink toenails vanish into his mouth and under his tongue. Nick's moans of pleasure and enthusiasm helped get me as wet as though it were my clit, and not my foot, he had between his lips. The taxi driver, who had probably seen much worse in his time, discreetly ignored the pair of us.

Nick's flat, not far from the West End, was an upscale bachelor pad. The living room was dominated by a large TV, a leather corner sofa and a six foot black-and-white photograph of a model wearing nothing but a pair of thigh-high boots.

Shakily, I undid the buckles of my shoes and stepped out of them: the wooden floor under my feet felt reassuring, like returning to dry land after you've been sailing. While Nick sniffed my shoes, I whipped my vest top over my head, kicked off my jeans and tore my bra and panties from my body. I was so eager to become that fantasy girl, naked but for a pair of £700 shoes. But first I would tease him a little.

I calmly took the shoes from Nick's hands and held them up in front of my tits. I let the straps trail all over my body, dug the stiletto heel into my skin, showing him the little mark it left on my flesh. Then I put the shoes on the coffee table where they glistened like the crown jewels and padded over to Nick. He began to ease his jeans over his hips while I pulled at his sweater, yanking it over his head. I took a step back to look at him and couldn't help sighing with pleasure and desire when I saw his body: it was beautifully slim, but well muscled, too. There was a scrawl of light brown hair on his chest and another on his smooth, pale balls. His pubic hair was trimmed neatly and framed a long, thick hard-on. I was wet and excited enough to fuck him there and then, but first I needed to change into my 'costume'.

'Please,' he said, his voice like a little boy's, 'please put your shoes on.'

'Not yet,' I said, enjoying the way the tables had been turned. In the shop, Nick had been the one with the credit card, barking orders, choosing the shoes, sweeping me into the cab. But now the power was all in my hands – or rather, *on* my feet.

I sat opposite him on that huge leather sofa. He

grabbed my leg and started to kiss my feet again, more voraciously this time, using his teeth as well as his tongue and exploring every inch of my foot from my toes to the sensitive spot on my ankle that was supposed to correlate to my clit.

I let my feet slide down so they were on his shoulders, pushing them back, and slowly parted my legs so that I could smell my own sweet musk and he could see my moist, glistening pussy. As he looked right into me, I saw his hard cock twitch and bounce and thought of a way to double his pleasure.

Slowly, I slid my feet down his chest, down his belly button and then I began to use my feet to tease his cock and balls. One foot gently tickling his balls, the other pressing on his perineum, then I touched my heels and toes together, arched my feet, and pulled this tunnel along the length of his dick, making him cry out in desire and frustration.

'That's enough for now,' I said, recognising the signs of a man who would erupt into a spontaneous orgasm unless I took a step back. What better time to concentrate on *my* pleasure?

So I figured it was my turn. I took one of the shoes in my hand and slid the silver strap over my vulva. With the soft side of the leather I rubbed back and forth, back and forth over my cunt, making my lips swell and my clit grow bigger and more intensely sensitive with each stroke. I wasn't shy about letting Nick know what this was doing to me. I moaned, threw my head back, parted my lips and rubbed a little harder, a little faster, letting the tension in my body build.

I sat up, held the other shoe to Nick's face, forced the heel of it between his lips: he wasted no time in sucking and licking it. Now that he'd cleaned it for me, I was ready to use it on myself. I took a deep breath, made sure he was watching and slid that long, plastic heel right inside my hole. It felt cool and smooth inside me.

I fucked myself with that shoe in front of Nick, drawing the heel in and out of my pussy, hard and fast, taking it all in right up to the wide end, parting my cunt lips and showing him just how I wanted him to fuck me – when I let him, that is.

'Nick, these shoes feel so good inside, it's almost a shame to wear them.'

'Oh God,' said Nick. 'Oh Jesus. Oh *please* . . .' I pulled the shoe out of me, held it up to the light. It was shiny with my juices.

'You want me to wear the shoes you bought me, Nick?' I said: the more I teased him, the bigger his dick seemed to grow. I was drunk on power and mad with lust. 'You want me to put these shoes on my pretty feet?'

He nodded, weakly, slack-jawed as I leapt off the sofa

and stepped back into my lovely new shoes. I did it slowly, fastening one buckle in one direction so that he had a good view of my arse and legs. Then when I did the other shoe, I turned my body around so he could see my tits bobbing just above my feet. When I stood up, tall, sexy, super-feminine, I felt like Wonder Woman.

He was sprawled on his sofa, dick in his hand, unable to stop wanking but trying desperately to keep himself from coming. His chest rippled as his rasping breath grew more urgent and shallow.

'You paid for these shoes. They feel good. What do you want me to do?'

'I want you to walk on me,' he growled. 'Up and down my spine. You don't know how good it makes me feel.'

With one hand leaning on the wall for support, I began to totter up and down Nick's back. As I walked, I saw old scars the size and shape of a sharp stiletto heel dragged across skin and realised that this wasn't the first time he had done this. But it only made me all the more determined that I would be the best he'd ever have.

I placed my feet either side of his body. He rolled over on to his back: I towered above him, staring at the beautiful face and body that lay bucking and twitching beneath me. Time to put us both out of our misery: I bent my legs at the knee, my pussy hovering over his hard-on for a few seconds and then he was inside me, finally satisfying the ache between my legs. I sat up straight on his erection and rode him hard.

Nick grabbed my ankles and pulled my feet up to his face, inhaling the shoe leather, mouth working wildly, sucking my toes, licking my ankles. I used one hand to keep my balance and the other to give me the stimulation I needed to come: I held my clit between my thumb and forefinger and pulled gently, giving it tiny tugs in perfect time with Nick's thrusting. When I forced the heel of my shoe across his neck, he pushed his hips upwards, his dick spearing me so hard I knew it was only a matter of seconds before I came. He bit down on the inside of my ankle and that was it: we came at the same time, an orgasm that started in my pussy and shot volts of electricity down to the tips of my jewelled toes.

We lay on the leather couch, bathed in sweat. I nuzzled into Nick's shoulder, but he wasn't kissing my hair, or stroking my cheek. He was staring at my feet: he was still thinking about the shoes. As my pulse rate returned to normal and the fog of lust dispersed, I could think more clearly. I realised it wasn't really me Nick was fucking – it was the shoes. They were his fetish – I was just a girl with pretty feet. It was the fuck of my life: no question. But when I got up and left his apartment, I knew I wouldn't see him again. I want someone to desire me because they adore the whole package – eyes, tits, hair, smile – as well as what I've got to offer below the knee.

I kept the shoes, though. I may be proud, but I'm not stupid.

HARD CELL

This one's a little controversial, but I like it . . . Not every woman is strong enough to allow herself to be dominated. But those who are . . . oh, they adore it.

This confession is not politically correct, and it did shock me. So let go of your preconceptions and imagine how it would feel if you were in this position. I think you'll get off on it . . . if you let yourself.

I lay on the narrow plank bed in the tiny cell: outside the daylight was fading but the single bulb illuminating the cell cast grey shadows across a grey room. Underneath the equally grey, drab prison uniform that we all had to wear in here, I was naked, skin pink and gold and brown, a secret splash of colour inside the institution where I spend my life. I liked the nakedness: the way the rough cotton contrasted with the softness of my skin turned me on.

And then the bell rang, a loud, dull chime that echoed throughout the long Victorian corridors. For most people, it was an unwelcome sign, as it meant that it was time for everyone to return to their cells for the evening. But for me, it was an erotic sound, one that made me shiver even more. He would be here any minute.

The thought of him made me writhe and wriggle on the grey blanket, the unlikely backdrop for the depraved sex games that had me coming night after night. The world of power-play and domination that Drew had introduced me to had to remain a secret: careers, reputations, even freedoms, were at stake. If we got caught, if someone came in and found me bound and gagged and being fucked so hard that I was almost in tears, well, you can imagine . . . it wouldn't exactly look good.

But we couldn't stop. I couldn't stop. When every grey day stretches out in front of you, the same for years and years, you need something to make you feel alive. And I loved the way he made me feel. I'd always been the one in control, a tough bitch who didn't put up with any shit. Well, you have to be to end up in here, I suppose. The first time I saw his six-foot bulk and he looked at me with contempt, I thought, okay, here we go, I've met my match in you. Just thinking about the way he spoke to me, the punishments he dealt out, had my hand working its way between my legs: I wanted to touch myself, get myself ready for his arrival, get myself ready for his cock.

As I heard his familiar footsteps in the corridor, I snatched my hand away. The rules of our power play meant

I'm not allowed to get myself off; only Drew is allowed to administer – or, indeed withhold – pleasure. And pain for that matter. Ah, the pleasure and pain – when Drew stands over me, barking orders, and my mind and body are fizzing with desire, I never know which is which.

The turn of the door handle meant he was here. He was really here! His tall, broad body dwarfed my own five-foot-one, eight-stone frame as I lay on the narrow bed, eyes downcast, not permitted to speak until he had spoken. He's teaching me respect, you see: showing me who's boss.

'Look who it is,' he said, in the rasping whisper that made the tiny hairs on the back of my neck stand on end and my nipples and clitoris swell in anticipation. 'It's time for your inspection. Now, can you please repeat the rules before we begin.'

I kept my voice to a whisper. In the corridor, inmates and guards shuffled along, doors clanked shut. Fuck, if they knew what was happening in here! If they *knew*!

'The rules!' Drew's voice came louder now.

I knew them by heart, of course, and delivered my little monologue in a low whisper. Repeating the rules focused my mind on the game, got me hot, got me ready.

'In this cell, you are my master and I am your slave. My sole purpose is to give you sexual pleasure. No matter how much I might want to, I am not allowed to derive pleasure from the act until you give your permission.'

(Who are we kidding, I thought: as if he's the only one that gets pleasure out of this.) 'Failure to obey your commands will result in my being punished. I must endure all punishments in complete silence.'

Drew nodded appreciatively. He was a big man (all over), and one of few words bar the commands he roared at me in the course of our games. Rock-solid, with close-cropped hair and a strong, jutting jawline. I noticed with a shiver that today he hadn't shaved so that the bristles on his chin were almost as dark as those on his head. The thought of his rasping stubble dragging across every inch of my own soft and tender flesh, scratching and burning me, made me wet.

'Take those horrible clothes off,' Drew commanded, interrupting my reverie. I was only too happy to obey: the first glimpse of my body always turned him on. It was the only time his façade cracked and for a few, brief seconds I had the balance of power. I could tell that it took all his self-control not to fuck me there and then. Aware of this, I unbuttoned my grey shirt to reveal the pink budding breasts I was so proud of, and unzipped the fly of my regulation grey trousers. You can't exactly get a bikini wax around here, but I'd trimmed my bush into a neat little goatee. Drew licked his lips.

It was cold in the cell: but I shivered from my desire as much as the chill. I stood naked in the middle of the tiny room while Drew walked around me, scrutinising my body, performing an almost military inspection. If he was looking for flaws, he would find none. I was proud of my body. His was a source of heat, and his warm breath caressed my collarbone, ears, nipples as he circled me. I savoured it knowing it would be the last soft, sensuous feeling I'd experience for a while.

Although I was naked, Drew remained fully-clothed. I know his body, know every inch of it: from his big cock with the jumping vein that swells just before he's about to come, to his dark, low-slung balls, to the curve of his back and his strong, broad shoulders. Knowing what his clothes are covering up but not being able to see is another way he teases me. By keeping his clothes on, he retains the power. I fucking love it.

'What shall I do with you today?' said Drew, but he wasn't really asking a question, he was wondering aloud which of the punishments he'd dish out this time. This was the best bit: the anticipation, not knowing. He fiddled with his belt buckle and then withdrew it from the belt loops, a clue as to what was coming next. My mind raced. Would it be a spanking session, putting me over his knee and smacking my bottom with a belt like a naughty school-girl? Would he force me to suck his cock, his huge erection a gag that muffled my own moans of pleasure?

'Okay, I've decided,' said Drew. As if he hadn't been

planning it all day! Probably tossed himself off in the shower thinking about it. In a rare moment of vulnerability, he'd confessed that sometimes he'd wank in the morning if he knew he was seeing me later. The games we played made him so horny, he was worried he'd come too soon. I loved knowing this, reassured that he too had to exercise enormous self-control.

'I can't trust you to keep still,' he said, 'So I think I'm going to have to restrain you.' And with that, he flexed the belt, and held it to my throat, so close I could smell the black leather and taste the metal of the buckle. The strap rested lightly across my neck, making me work harder for every inhalation, my breath coming in audible sighs.

'Lie back on the bed,' said Drew.

I climbed on to the tiny plank bed, the grey prison issue blanket scratching the skin on my arse.

'Raise your arms above your head.'

This showed my tits off so Drew could see how erect my nipples were. My breasts rose and fell, begging for his touch. He wasn't going to give me the satisfaction – yet. His face remained impassive, expressionless, but his deep breathing and the bulge in his trousers confirmed that he was enjoying his role as master just as much as I got off on being his slave. With confident, strong hands, Drew bound me to the iron bars of the single bed with his belt, looping the leather around my wrists, finally pulling tight and fastening it together by buckling it on its smallest hole. I pulled at the belt, testing how tightly I was bound. There was hardly any room to move. I was no longer in control of my own body.

He forced one knee in between my legs, spreading them as wide as they'd go, looking at my cunt. We could play all the games in the world, and I can say 'no', pretend I don't like it, but right there between my legs was evidence of just how much I was enjoying myself: you can act along and pretend you don't like it when you do, but the sight and smell of a swollen, dripping pussy and a quivering, engorged clitoris never lie. He leaned in, inhaled.

'Smells like a slut's getting turned on,' he said.

Then he forced my legs a little further apart, a little further than was comfortable, pulling the muscles in my thighs until they begged for mercy, but I bit my lip: the wider my legs were spread, the more exposed and vulnerable my pussy was, and the wetter it got.

'Oh, is that too much for you?' said Drew with a sneer.

And with his big strong hands he pushed hard on the insides of my knees, forcing me almost to do the splits. The ache in my thighs became an acute pain as he put his face between my thighs and slid his tongue in and out of my aching pussy, making it like a little cock, in and out, in and out. What I really wanted was for him to lick my clitoris which was swollen and frustrated, but I wouldn't have asked him to even if I'd been allowed. Then, as my legs began to cramp, I broke.

'Please, it hurts, I can't take it any more!' I cried.

'Yes you can,' said Drew, my pussy muffling his words.

'I *can't*,' I said although I knew I could and I knew that the more I endured now, the greater the release at the end of it. I began bucking and writhing, partly because of the pain and partly because I knew Drew liked the way my flesh jiggled when I struggled. The leather strap bit into the flesh of my wrists. I knew there would be red welts on my skin when the belt was removed but the tiny pain biting into me felt so good I couldn't stop moving.

'Look at you,' he said, 'Unable to control yourself. Can't lie still for a minute. Well, we'll see if you can control *this*,' and with that, he delivered a sharp, tiny slap to the side of my breast. The sting gave way to a burning sensation and I bent my head to watch as the flesh of my tit wobbled then stayed still. A red handprint began to form on my skin: as his mark on me grew more pronounced, my nipples grew harder and darker, too. Drew continued to slap my breasts, both hands flat and stinging on my skin, until my chest was on fire. I let it happen, let the blood rush to my breasts, swelling them, making them more sensitive until suddenly it happened, and the pleasure crossed the line into pain.

'Mercy!' I wailed, unable to bear the smacking for a second longer. 'Mercy!'

Drew put his lips to my nipples, used his tongue to cool the smarting skin, but his tender kisses were a new form of torture. He knew that once my nipples had been sucked, I wanted, needed, to be fucked. And I knew his game; it was far too soon for him to give me that kind of satisfaction. If I wanted him to penetrate me, or play with my clit, I was going to have to start begging.

'Please,' I whimpered. 'Please . . .'

'Please what?' said Drew, even though he knew perfectly well that I was begging for a soft tongue on my clitoris, the sweet relief of orgasm.

'Please let me come. Please make me come. Please let me come. Please make me come. Please please please please please . . .'

'Come?' said Drew, contemptuously. 'We're not even close to that yet.'

I didn't answer him back but thrust my aching, erect clitoris towards him, hoping it made its own silent and irresistible plea for his tongue.

'I'm going to untie you now,' he said, unfastening the belt buckle and unthreading the leather strap from the iron bars of the bed. 'But that doesn't mean you can move unless I say so. If you move again, I won't let you come this evening. Do you understand?'

I nodded, eyes wide and serious. He'd never threatened to withhold my climax before. That was a chance I couldn't take. I made a vow to be extra obedient for the rest of our session.

He motioned for me to stand up. I obeyed. To my surprise, he wound his belt around my ribcage, something he'd never done before: he was so much bigger than me that he could get the whole thing around me twice, binding my tits so that the nipples poked out between two straps of leather. He flicked my left nipple, then the other. They swelled and darkened, aching for more of his touch. He bent down and took first my left nipple, then my right, in his lips and swirled his tongue around, gently nibbled and sucked on them, making me wish he'd do the same to my clit.

Instead, he swung me roughly around, so that I was standing with my back to him. He pulled on the belt from behind, turning it into a little harness. My arms hung limply by my sides. It would have been so easy to slide my hand between my legs and bring myself off to the climax I so badly needed, but I didn't dare. I could do it, sure, but it would be nothing compared to the intense, fiery peak Drew would be able to bring out. So I tried to concentrate on the sensation that was building up in my chest, making me struggle for breath, torturing and distorting the most sensitive curves of my body. I settled for squeezing my thighs together as tightly as I could, subtly squeezing my pussy lips so the friction would give my clit a secret massage.

With his free hand, Drew unzipped his fly and freed his cock, his beautiful, fat cock that I loved to look at so much. Not being able to see it was all part of my torture. He lifted me up on to the bed, then let go of the belt and bent me double so that I was half-suffocating in the scratchy grey blankets, my arse sticking up in the air. Drew parted my buttcheeks and spat on my arsehole before grabbing the belt between my shoulder blades and yanking my body upright again. His saliva on my anus was warm and moist and was quickly followed by his dick, teasing the entrance to my arse, a huge hard-on forcing its way into a tiny tight hole. I braced myself for the split second of searing pain, biting so hard on my lip that I drew blood. With one forceful thrust he penetrated me, his dick filling the whole of my inside. Holding me by the makeshift harness so tight that the circulation in my tits was almost cut off, he thrust deep into me, sometimes so forcefully that my feet left the bed and I was riding his dick, like a tiny jockey mounted on a thoroughbred racehorse, a racehorse that was out of control. The sheer size of his dick up my arse and the tingling in my tits was so intense that, for a while, I was distracted from the yearning in my clit.

'Do you like this?' he snarled in my ear. It was a trick

question. Say yes, and he'd do it harder. Say no, and he'd do it harder. Instead of giving him a direct answer, I repeated my earlier plea.

'Please, please let me come,' I wailed.

'What did I tell you about self-control?' Drew was nearly shouting now; I was grateful that noise didn't carry very well in these thick-walled, Victorian institutions. He pulled his cock out of me so suddenly that it was almost as intense as the first penetration had been. He unbuckled the belt, whipped it away from my skin. Sensation began to return to my breasts, but I barely had time to register this before he flung me face-down on to the bed and brought the belt down on my arse like a whip, the buckle sending white-hot pain to my skin one, twice, three times. I screamed into the pillow, starting rubbing against the blanket, my clitoris getting the stimulation I needed from the scratchy fibres. It would hurt like hell in the morning, but I didn't care. I needed to come, and I needed to come now.

Drew spread my legs again and I moaned, sure he was going to fuck my arsehole again, when I had never needed him inside my cunt so badly. But when his dick probed my hole again, it was my pussy this time. He drove into my cunt with the same mercilessness that he'd used on my arse, but this time I was grateful, needed it, couldn't have it hard enough. It didn't take long: only ten, maybe twelve, thrusts before the combination of the blanket on my clit and the pounding in my pussy made me come, hot waves of energy radiating through my body like ripples on a pond. Sore, sensitive and exhausted, I let myself go limp from head to toe.

Drew's huge, heavy body hovered over me and his orgasm was close behind mine.

As he came, he forgot who was in control: it was his turn to surrender to the way my body made him feel.

'Baby, you feel so good . . . so good.' He pulled out of me, rolled me over, buried his head on the breasts that were covered with the scars and welts of our lovemaking session and finally, finally gave me a long kiss on the lips.

We lay in each other's arms while what little light there was outside faded: our breath made mist that condensed and made smoky trails in the cold air.

'Lights out in ten minutes,' came the call from the corridor.

'I'd better go,' I said, getting up from my lover's arms and slipping back into my sharp, black, workplace suit. 'My night shift staff will be arriving soon and I've got to go through the usual drill with a new screw . . . and it wouldn't do for me to be seen in here.'

'Same time tomorrow?' said Drew, settling down in his cell for the night.

'Same time tomorrow,' I said, winking and letting

myself out of the cell. I locked him in for the night, walked down the long, deserted corridor to my office, straightened my hair and prepared to resume my other life as governor of the prison.

STATUESQUE

This story will help you work up an appetite in more ways than one . . .

There are two great sensual pleasures in life: food and sex. I've always had a healthy appetite for both, but never thought that my passion for food would lead me to the best sex of my life.

It was a couple of summers ago now. I was single, and I had a bad case of wanderlust. I needed a holiday but the only one that my friends were up for was the lying-around-on-a-beach kind. That's not for me. I like to do stuff on holiday, experience new cultures, explore different ways of living. Flipping idly through the travel supplements one Sunday, a tiny square of newsprint caught my eye. It was an advert with a pen-and-ink drawing of a vine-covered villa, unmistakably Italian. 'Learn to cook like the Italians,' the advert read. 'Week-long residential course in villa in Umbria. Accommodation provided. Singles, couples and groups of all ages and abilities welcome.'

I knew then that I'd found the ideal trip: staying in beautiful countryside, indulging my taste for Italian wine and learning to cook the kind of food I loved to eat in restaurants but never quite managed to pull off at home. And I liked the idea that there'd be a good mix of people. Knowing there'll be other singletons to knock about with is always reassuring when you're a woman travelling alone. And if one of those singletons happens to be an attractive young man . . . well, so much the better.

The night before my departure, I packed my bags with a sense of real anticipation and adventure. Instead of the usual bikinis and low-cut tops, I packed elegant, floaty dresses, appropriate for sophisticated dining with like-minded foodies. And then, at the last minute, I threw in my bikinis. It was Italy, after all, and I didn't want to waste any sunshine.

I took a taxi from Pisa airport and we drove out through the city's suburbs and into another world. It was like something out of a romantic movie: the whole countryside stretched out as far as I could see, shimmering shades of green and gold. Wild olive trees lined the sides of the road and the scent of wild basil and garlic wafted through the air. Every new, fresh scent relaxed me, made me feel more sensual and alive. I realised how long it had been since I'd breathed air this clean, smelt anything this natural and beautiful.

The first sight of the villa was breathtaking. It was terracotta red, set in acres of rolling hills and flanked by vineyards that stretched for miles and miles. I was shown to my bedroom by a smiling middle-aged woman who introduced herself in broken English as Emilia, the lady of the house and tutor for the week. The accommodation was basic: burnt orange walls, a single bed covered with a white sheet and a small wardrobe. But I'd come here for the kitchen, and what a kitchen it was. Spread with all the produce you could find, stocked with fine vintage wines, and in the middle was a huge, ancient pine table where Emilia explained we would eat every night. I was like a kid in a candy store, nosing around in cupboards and sniffing fresh herbs and exotic oils. I was in foodie heaven.

One by one, the other guests arrived: they were almost all English, and a good bunch, nice and friendly, and that night over a few bottles of the local *vino* the group got chatting and I realised they were as keen to learn and have a good holiday as I was. But they were all couples apart from two female friends in their late forties. While I was happy to have found cookery companions who shared my passion for good food as well as my sense of humour, I couldn't help but be a little disappointed at the lack of single men. Just someone to flirt with would have added an extra frisson to my vacation. The Italian idyll would have been the perfect place to have a little holiday fling. Anyone who doesn't find the Umbrian landscape sensual, evocative and romantic must have a heart of stone. As the evening wore on, however, I laughed and drank so much that I forgot about sex. I went to bed happy, overstuffed and looking forward to a fabulous week.

I woke early the next morning with the Tuscan sun beaming through a chink in the shutters. It had been hot enough for me to sleep naked, and the room was sultry, the cotton sheets cool against my skin and the terracotta floor tiles deliciously warm and dry beneath my feet. Grabbing a chocolate brown swimsuit with cutaway sides, I wrapped myself in a white towel and padded through the villa to the pool.

The warmth of the sun wrapped my body in a hug like a lover. I'm a real sun-worshipper and I'd underestimated how much I'd been deprived of strong great Mediterranean sunshine. The early morning rays shone gently on my back and legs, warming my insides pleasantly. It felt like a kiss does when you haven't had any contact with a lover for a long time: you bury those feelings but then someone kisses you, and woosh! Suddenly you're alive, alert and ready for anything.

After my swim, I tucked into a hearty breakfast of fruit and yoghurt, covered in honey from the estate's beehives. Emilia and her husband, Enzo, talked us through the day's lessons: we would learn how to make pasta from scratch. I spent the whole day making a complete mess of things and we all ended up covered in flour and water with bits in our hair. Some of the couples kissed each other's messy noses, tenderly wiping their partner's faces clean. Watching them, I felt a pang of something that was part jealousy, part arousal.

By the time we prepared the evening meal, we'd all mastered the art of making perfect pasta. We dined on the food we'd spent the day preparing. When I went to bed, I lay awake, listening to the crickets chirrup. I couldn't sleep: too full of food and wine. So I slipped on the only nightie I had brought with me – a midnight-blue silk negligee – and stepped outside for some fresh air. I took a stroll in the Italianate garden. Under the moonlight, ivy clambered over statues and the leaves of potted plants cast eerie shadows. I let my fingers trail over a statue, a replica of Michelangelo's David, cupping his smooth buttocks. Even looking at his lean, muscular athletic thighs made me think it would be nice to have my own legs entwined with a pair like that. I let my hand trace the warm skin of my collarbone, closed my eyes, imagined it was a lover's caress. I allowed myself a private smile at the disproportionately small size of David's lunchbox which perhaps the great sculptor chipped away at accidentally.

On my way back to bed, I glimpsed another statue,

this one naked and standing with its back to me, facing out over the moonlit landscape. And I *swear* I saw the statue move, the marble torso twist and stretch. I rubbed my eyes, looked again, but saw nothing. Too much wine, I thought. Time to go to bed before I had any more hallucinations. As I drifted off to sleep that night, I imagined that one of those statues had come to life, a white, perfectly sculpted male body, strong enough to pick me up, take me in his arms and make slow, tender love to me. When I woke up the next morning, the sheets between my legs were sticky.

I swam forty laps of the pool before breakfast to work up an appetite for the day's workshop. I came out of the water, and began to dry myself, admiring my developing tan. I sensed someone watching me from the corner of my eye, but when I whipped my head around sunlight blinded me, and when my sight had recovered, there was no one there. But I felt a shiver – as though I were not alone. As though there were a man close to me.

Another day, another recipe. We were learning how to make Italian salads: when the ingredients were this delicious and fresh, they almost made themselves. We spent the day drizzling olive oil and balsamic vinegar over roasted vegetables, tearing mozzarella and slicing avocados. When I thought no one was looking, I'd lick my fingers and allow my eyes to close for a moment, pretending that they were a man's hands, a lover's fingers. There was something about this place that left me in a state of permanent arousal.

At lunchtime, we all sat by the pool, taking our salads and our wine al fresco, the way such food was meant to be enjoyed. Dazzled by the midday sun, I went inside to fetch my sunglasses. As I walked along the corridor to my room, I had that feeling again: that someone was watching me. That someone was there. This time, when I turned around, I was rewarded with a sight that took my breath away.

A few metres away, wearing only a pair of jeans and holding a large bag of flour on broad, muscular shoulders, was a young man as perfectly sculpted as the statues in Emilia's garden. 'Hello?' I said, and took a step towards him, but he disappeared through a door like a startled deer. I returned to the rest of the group, still not entirely sure that I'd seen anyone at all. Was I so sexually frustrated that I imagined statues coming to life? Had I had too much sun as well as wine?

The next evening, I walked through the garden again. As before, I allowed my hands to fondle the 'flesh' of the male statues, hoping that their real-life counterpart would materialise. But I saw no sign of him, didn't even sense his presence like I had before. That night I lay in my bed, unable to sleep. My hands found their way between my legs, and slowly, I slid my finger in between my pussy lips and used the moisture I knew would be in there to lubricate my clitoris and made languid, stroking motions until a gentle orgasm flowed through my body. Once I'd come, I was asleep within seconds.

But with the morning came my first real sighting of him: when I approached the pool for my morning swim, he was there. My first thought was, 'Thank goodness I'm not going mad. He really exists!' My second was 'Oh my God, what a body.' He put the statues to shame and judging by the bulge in his pants he had far more to be proud of. 'Hello,' I said casually, hoping that my quavering voice didn't betray my desire. 'We haven't met. I'm Kelly. Have I seen you about the place before? I'm sure I have. In the garden the other night, and then in the corridor? It's nice to see you in daylight.'

I was gabbling now, nervously trying to hide the fact that I had masturbated over the thought of this man just a few hours ago. Now that I could see his face clearly, it was obvious he was about my age, late twenties: a smooth, oval face was topped off by a mop of wavy, darkest brown hair that curled at the nape of his neck. He had perspired while he worked and sweat wound his hair into tight, damp coils around his forehead.

His face showed absolute bafflement, but broke into a gorgeous smile, pink fleshy lips parting to reveal even white teeth and a flash of pink tongue. 'Cristiano,' he said shyly, and then, '*Mi dispiace* . . . no English.'

He held out his hand. I had to walk across hot flagstones to touch it. He jumped a little when our hands met: clearly he too sensed the chemical reaction that took place between us, a charge that made the hair all over my body stand up on end and caused me to shiver, despite the strong sun. I turned back to the pool and dropped my towel, conscious that he might be watching me, aware that I was looking good after a few days' fresh food and daily swims, hoping that he saw the graceful arc I made when I dived into the water. The cool water dampened down the stirrings of lust that had begun to warm my body, but with every stroke I imagined Cristiano's body and face, inches away from mine. I pictured him leaning in for a kiss . . . I envisaged that perfect upper torso raised over mine while we fucked. When I emerged from the pool, he was nowhere to be seen. But once again, I felt his eyes on mine and I knew that he was there, hiding in a doorway or behind a window, observing me, drinking me in. I made sure that I stretched out, the tight lycra of my swimsuit clinging to the curves of my body, the outlines of my nipples poking pertly through the thin brown fabric.

'I see you meet my boy,' said Emilia later that day while I learned how to make ciabatta bread. 'Cristiano. He work here for the summer but he no have any English. He too lazy to try! But he is a good boy.' Was it me, or did I detect a glimmer in the old lady's eye that showed me she knew just what I wanted to do with her son?

'Why doesn't he eat with us?' I said. 'Doesn't he like our cooking?'

Emilia laughed. 'He shy,' she said. 'That's all.'

Because Cristiano, and his beautiful body, occupied my thoughts entirely, I burned my first attempt at making bread, and my second fared little better. My concentration was somewhere other than baking perfect loaves. I walked every corridor of the villa that evening, and paced every metre of the garden, hoping for just another glimpse but he was nowhere to be seen. Short of asking Emilia of his whereabouts and revealing my interest to his own mother, I had no way of finding him. I didn't even know if he lived here or travelled in to work every day.

It wasn't surprising that that night, I woke up tangled in sheets which were bathed with my sweat, crying out in frustration. From the tension in my body, the pulse between my legs and the position of my hands on my vulva I could tell that I'd been dreaming about Cristiano and touching myself while I slept: I had woken before I'd had the chance to reach the orgasm I so obviously craved.

I'd made myself so hot and thirsty that I had to have a glass of water. I wrapped myself in the bedlinen and wandered down to the kitchen, felt for the tap and filled a glass with icy cold water which flooded my body with sweet relief. I stood at the open fridge and grabbed a juicy strawberry, bit into it, refreshed myself. I was now wide awake and knew there was no point going back to bed. Instead, I poured myself a glass of thick, sticky vin santo and sat down at the kitchen table.

And there he was in the doorway: Cristiano. Silhouetted against the moonlight, his lithe body filled the doorframe. He was naked. Everything was outlined by the pale blue light: the slim, toned hips, the soft bulge of his muscular thighs, the down of his pubic hair and a long, thick dick hanging down between his legs. He was more beautiful and more perfectly carved than any statue I'd ever seen.

We remained silent. What was the point of speaking? My Italian was no better than his English. I was suddenly very conscious that I wore only a sheet. A thin layer of cotton was all that lay between my soft, creamy skin and his hard, bronzed body.

Cristiano sat down opposite me at the table and took a sip of my glass of wine. Then he looked at me, his eyes black pools, and picked up a strawberry and put it into his mouth. He sucked the tip, his pink lips wrapping themselves around the ripe red fruit, his tongue making a little shelf for it to rest on. He licked it, savoured it, chewed and swallowed. He licked his lips, picked up another strawberry. With long, slender fingers he pulled the stalk off the top and then placed the berry very gently between my own lips. I let him push it a little further, shut my eyes and kissed the strawberry, imagined that the soft round tip of the fruit was his dick that I was taking between my lips. I bit down, slicing it in two: Cristiano took the other half and ate, smiling at me. In the moonlight I could see the faint red traces of the fruit's juices on his lips.

Sure now that I wouldn't be rejected, I leaned forward and with the tip of my tongue, I tickled his upper lip, licking off the sweet liquid and tasting something else too, a salty, masculine musk that was pure Cristiano. Slowly he parted his lips, let his tongue touch mine. We spent what seemed like hours seated at that table kissing one another, investigating each other's mouths gently, sweet and salty tastes.

When I brought my hands to his head and ran my fingers through his curls the bedsheet that was wrapped around my body fell open. I let it. Cristiano's hands, when they slowly reached out to touch my breasts, were hot and dry. Our lips remained locked together, but his hands moved swiftly, brushing every inch of my flesh as though searching for knowledge of me, like he were reading my body the way a blind man reads Braille. He felt each breast individually, fingers deftly working nipples, he stroked my underarms and the sensitive flesh along my sides. And everything he did was in slow, slow motion stoking my desire far more powerfully than any man I'd ever known. Rather than forcing my lust, he let it build up a head of steam all on its own. His secret was simple. Cristiano didn't have any unusual moves: he didn't put his hand or lips anywhere other men hadn't touched me. He leaned in closer, his knee touching mine but that perfect torso remaining tantalisingly away from my body. What made the difference between good sex and the obliterating feeling that was almost an out-of-body experience was the patient, almost unbearably beautiful pace at which he did it.

When my arousal was beginning to build to a powerful crescendo, Cristiano stood up. He placed his hands on my shoulders and raised me up so that I stood naked in the kitchen and trembling all over, craving more of his tender touch yet wildly excited by the unknown prospect of what would happen next. '*Bellisma*,' he whispered, tucking a strand of hair behind my ear. '*Ti voglio, ma primo, mangiamo*.' I had no idea what he was saying, of course, but his tone was urgent, his voice low, and his intentions were clear. He turned his gaze to the huge, old-fashioned refrigerator and opened the door. The artificial light flooded the kitchen and illuminated the big, thick, hard-on that was a work of art in itself, and his finely chiselled butt cheeks. I was a little surprised when Cristiano then gathered together a variety of Emilia's cooking supplies in his arms. A basket of fruit. A huge bottle of olive oil. A pot of yoghurt. A jar of honey.

He picked me up by the hips and sat me on the edge of the old pine table. Its rugged warmth felt pleasant beneath my buttocks. He took his bunch of grapes and dipped each one in honey. Gently pushing me to indicate that I was to lie down, he then placed the grapes all over my body: one between my tits, another one on my collarbone, another on each hand. Each one felt as cool as a kiss, and I could feel them, sticky and sexy, teasing my erogenous zones.

Then he slowly knelt over me and kissed every inch of my body, eating the fruit, licking it, making murmurs of appreciation as he teased and tantalised my skin. By the time he had eaten every grape, I was twitching and shivering with desire.

Taking his lead, I reached into the pot of yoghurt, smothered some on his chest and reached up to lick it off, my tongue enjoying the taste of the rich, creamy liquid and the salty tang of his skin.

He placed a strawberry between the lips of my pussy, left it there, teasing me. It made me crave penetration.

'Please,' I said, 'I want you inside me, I need to feel you inside me.' But he didn't understand.

Cristiano put a generous serving of honey on his dick and I turned on to all fours, knelt on the kitchen table, oblivious to the discomfort in my knees. I wanted to take as much of him as possible in. He was murmuring to himself in Italian: although I didn't understand a single word, his body language and the tone of his voice told me all I needed to know about the effect I was having on him.

He took his dick away from my lips, hoisted me up by my hips and pulled my body from behind so that I was face down on the table, my legs dangling over the side. I spread my legs, certain that he was going to fuck me – he had to, now he'd got me so turned on. But he didn't fuck me; instead, he drizzled olive oil on to my skin, the golden liquid making a long rivulet down my spine. His hands massaged the oil into my skin, melting away any tension that remained in my body. He then poured oil into his hands, massaged my feet and worked his way up my legs, slowly, slowly rubbing towards my inner thighs but not quite touching them as far as my pussy lips.

Cristiano turned his attention to my arse, pouring more and more olive oil on to the now very soft skin, making circles with his fists and pummelling the flesh there, making the blood flow to my whole pelvis. I relaxed under his masterful touch, but got a shock when he parted the cheeks of my arse. Oh God! What was he doing? I had my answer soon enough when he slid a finger into my anus. Actually right into it! I'd never known a man touch me there before but as soon as I felt his finger circling my arsehole, I knew I loved it. He slid his finger in and out of my hole, softly at first, easing away any tension I held there.

He waited until he was sure I was comfortable with his finger in my arse and then slid his dick into my aching pussy. He kept twisting the finger in my ass at the same time as he plunged his hard-on into my cunt: I could feel his balls banging against my thighs and the rasp of his curly pubic hair tickle the oily small of my back. I had never felt so full up, so overwhelmed, so well and truly *fucked*, in my whole life. When I finally came, my pussy and arse both squeezed hard around his dick and finger. I felt searing heat flood my cunt and rise up to my cheeks and chest.

As soon as my orgasm subsided, Cristiano pulled out of me and stuck his dick in my olive-oil lubed arsehole, once, twice, three times. The first time made me gasp with pain. The second one felt amazing, and on the third thrust he came, shouting in Italian. I felt his hot cum spurt into my arsehole. I felt a sweet relief as he pulled his dick out of me and let the cum spill out and roll down the back of my legs.

His fine, dusky-coloured dick was magnificent even when limp. My body, too was limp and exhausted:

Cristiano scooped me into his arms and I let myself flop there like a wilted flower. He took me over to the pool, carried me down the steps into the water which was cold even though the night was warm. There we splashed and licked each other clean of the food, oil and sex juices that were smeared all over the pair of us. We staggered back as the sun rose around 5 a.m. Cristiano gave me one last slow kiss as he walked back to whichever secret part of the villa he slept in. I returned to my room and fell asleep instantly.

I was woken at 9 a.m. by an irate Emilia, telling me off for missing breakfast and being late for the morning's session. I pulled on my clothes, mumbled an apology and wondered if last night had been a dream – an intensely erotic, and wonderfully satisfying dream. Cristiano was nowhere to be seen. On my way to the kitchen, I passed the pool. I saw a slick of olive oil shimmering on the surface of the water, and a set of oily footprints heading towards the terrace, and knew that it had all been real.

THE LURE OF THE GREASEPAINT

Some people say that in the right dress, and wearing the right make-up, you can take on a persona totally different to your own. If that's true, then the more extreme the costume, the more outrageously you'll behave when you wear it. Goodness knows we all have an outfit that helps us behave a certain sexual way with confidence, be it a nymphette in knee-socks or a super-bitch in a power suit. But as the girls who told me this story found, the really wild stuff starts when you take the costume off . . .

My best friend Tania and I have always hung out with an arty, creative crowd. We share a house with five other students, and there's always someone with a photography project on the go, a band to audition for, or some avant-garde performance art to participate in. What's the point of being a student if you don't throw yourself into every opportunity and experience?

Tania came back from uni one day clutching a flyer

appealing for budding starlets to take part in an independent art-house film. 'Look, Jade,' she said, waving the leaflet in my face. 'Female actors wanted for party scene in short film. Expenses and fee paid.'

'It sounds great,' I said to Tania. 'There's just one thing. We're not actresses.'

'Well we are now,' she replied mischievously. 'We'll tell him we're drama students. Getting paid to dress up and muck about? It's too good an opportunity to miss.'

Before I could say anything else, she'd called Darrel, the film's director. It turned out he was a final-year film student making a short film about a wild, decadent party set in the 1930s. His enthusiasm for the film was catching, and Tania and I both relished the prospect of donning the feathers, furs and silks of such a glamorous period. Darrel explained that the parts didn't have any dialogue, but who cares when you get to raid the dressing-up box? After we emailed him a photo of ourselves, he called us back to say we'd got the job and to keep the next weekend free for filming.

Darrel had found a fabulous location for the day's filming: an old, art-deco restaurant off an Edinburgh side-street. The interior had fabulous swirled oak panelling, potted palms and fans on the ceiling: it was like taking a step back in time to the jazz age. The tables were loaded with piles of fruit on golden platters and plates of oysters on ice. Champagne was poured into crystal champagne saucers. We tried some and were disappointed to find that it was only sparkling apple juice.

Our first stop was hair and make-up, where our hair was set in elaborate waves sculpted close to our heads. Our eyes and eyebrows were emphasised with dramatic make-up and our lips painted with a glossy plum stain.

In the mirror I looked at Tania's reflection, her blonde hair and lavish make-up transforming her from the fresh-faced girl I knew into a vamp from bygone era. When my own metamorphosis was complete I barely recognised my face in the mirror: the big, round eyes of a 1930s screen siren stared back at me.

'You look incredible,' said Tania, catching my eye in the glass.

'So do you,' I replied.

Next stop was wardrobe, where rows of shimmering, floor-length gowns hung on rails. I chose a figure-hugging dress of emerald-green silk, with a cutaway back that was nearly-but-not-quite guilty of displaying my butt cleavage to the world. There was no question of underwear in *this* dress! As I took off all my clothes to slip into it, I was aware of Tania watching me. Her gaze was more intense than I had witnessed before, or perhaps it was over-emphasised by the make-up that rimmed her eyes. Well, I thought, anything that helps us get into character can only be a good thing. I finished my look with a pair of silver leather slingback shoes and a silver fake fox-fur stole that I wrapped around my bare shoulders.

Meanwhile Tania slipped a wine-red gown over her own head: she too realised that twenty-first-century underwear was incompatible with the clingy dresses of yesteryear and I caught a glimpse of her slim, lightly tanned body, curvier than mine, and with a neatly trimmed fuzz of blonde hair on her pudenda. I looked away, suddenly shy. The wardrobe girl handed her a pair of black patent shoes and a black fur stole, and placed a feather plume in Tania's hair. Our costumes complete, we looked at each other in awed silence.

'You look incredible, Jade,' said Tania, repeating her earlier compliment.

'You too!' I giggled. 'Who is this glamorous, exotic stranger?'

'Oh Jade, I *know!*' she replied. 'I feel like I'm not myself in these clothes, like I'm capable of having all these wild adventures that I wouldn't normally dare to. Do you know what I mean?' I recognised the twinkle in her eye and her tone of voice: she was . . . she was *flirting* with me!

'Well, this should be fun,' I said, a little unnerved. 'Let's go on to the set and see who else is there.'

When we made our way on to the set, we found an array of dazzling characters whose exotic, opulent costumes made our own outfits look positively tame. As well as several young men in white-tie and tails, we were startled to see a dozen or so women dressed as fan dancers in skimpy attire that left nothing to the imagination: smatterings of sequins on their nipples and bushes were all they wore. Two men, totally nude, reclined together on a chaise longue in the corner of the room. A woman in scarlet lipstick wore an unbuttoned leopard-print coat, a pair of high heels and nothing else.

Tania and I exchanged a glance that was part alarm, part fascination. 'Just what kind of film is this?' she gasped.

We didn't have to wait long for our answer. Tania identified Darrel as the tall, good-looking guy in a dark corner, deep in discussion with a lighting technician. He looked out of place in his jeans and sweatshirt, but confident and capable. He clapped his hands for silence and the assembled cast and crew turned to look at him expectantly.

'Thank you all for coming here to take part in my humble little film,' he began. 'I know that you're all giving up your time today, and that some of you have never acted before' – was it my imagination, or did he shoot a secret wink at Tania and me?

'This, as you know, is the orgy scene, the final shot of the film.'

Had we heard him right? *Orgy* scene? He certainly hadn't said anything about a gang-bang when he hired us!

I looked at Tania, but she was staring open-mouthed at Darrel, clearly as shocked as I was.

'Don't worry!' he went on. 'Most of you won't have to do anything very sexually explicit, we've got hardcore drama students for that,' and he gestured towards the half-naked group in the corner, who waved with a confident insouciance as if pretending to have sex naked on camera in fancy dress was something they did every day – hey, for all I knew, maybe it was.

'The rest of you will just be milling about in the background, watching, maybe eating and drinking.' As soon as he said this, I felt a little disappointed and was astonished to realise I'd have been ready to join in the orgy scene. Perhaps it was the electric atmosphere, or perhaps it was the fact that in my costume I felt like a wild, wanton woman. Either way, I felt bold and – I'll admit it – more than a little horny. But I didn't have time to dwell on this feeling, as Darrel ushered all of us on to our marks.

He ordered the people wearing the least clothes to drape themselves around each other on an enormous, curved sofa that dominated the middle of the room. I doubted that there was room on the velvet seat for all ten of them, but as bodies and limbs became entangled, they proved that indeed there was.

'You two look good together,' he said, gesturing towards me and Tania. 'Nice contrast of blonde and brunette. You can stand looking over them. With a glass of champagne in your hand, naturally.'

'What do we do?' asked Tania, voicing my own anxieties.

'Just act,' said Darrel. Up close he was really good-looking: his dark hair brushed his collarbone and fell into his eyes when he spoke. For some crazy reason it made me want to tuck it behind his ear. 'I imagine that if you *were* at an orgy, you wouldn't be able to take your eyes off the action. Just watch them, sip your champagne, do what comes naturally to you. If it's any consolation, people will probably be more interested in what's going on in front of you than in your own performances!'

'Sure,' said Tania, with a nervous laugh. 'No worries.'

Next thing we knew, the lights blazed, and Darrel shouted 'Action.' A string quartet started to play a jazz tune and the mass of bodies in front of us came to life, arms, arses, tits, backs, legs and tongues interlaced in what looked like the throes of passion. All I could do was stare, open-mouthed. I wasn't acting: I was genuinely fascinated. How could they be acting? Surely they were all turned on: you can't roll around in a sea of naked flesh and not enjoy it just a little bit. I felt myself blush and was grateful for the thick stage make-up covering my cheeks and hiding my embarrassment. Tania let out a sigh next to me, I could tell that she was starting to feel something, too.

'Okay guys, that was great,' said Darrel, gesturing to the heap of bodies writhing beneath us. 'But you two, I need a little more movement there after all – I know you're transfixed, but . . . can you come here for a second, girls?'

Tania and I wandered over to Darrel's chair. 'Listen, Tania, Jade. You two look so good together it's a shame to waste it,' he said. 'I know this isn't what we discussed, but is there any way I could persuade you to spice it up a little? It would make the whole scene so much more intense. Just a kiss, only acting. Nothing too graphic: you wouldn't be taking your clothes off or anything like that.'

My mind was reeling. Sure, what I'd seen was making me horny, but I'd been thinking about some girl-on-guy action. And later. And off camera. But then again, there was something special and a little weird about the way Tania was making me feel today. I thought of the slender curves of her naked body that I'd seen an hour or so before in wardrobe, and as the image of her breasts and belly swum before my eyes, suddenly I knew that I wanted to kiss her more than anything. But she was my best friend. What if I said it was cool and Tania was turned off by the idea? Our friendship would be ruined.

Luckily once again Tania came to my rescue. 'I thought you'd never ask,' she said, with a cheeky smile in Darrel's direction.

'Er, yes,' I stammered, shocked at my best friend's unprecedented bravado. 'Er, that's fine by me, too.'

'Great,' said Darrel. 'Again, just do what comes naturally, a little kiss, not too graphic: I want some movement so that the audience has plenty to look at, but I don't want you to upstage the main sex scene.'

I looked over to where a beautiful woman knelt on all fours, naked but for a single silk stocking and a peacock feather clasped between her butt cheeks.

'I don't think there's much chance of upstaging *her*,' I said. The three of us laughed, the ice broken.

'Off you go then, ladies,' said Darrel, and then, 'for what it's worth, I think you both look horny as hell.' And with those words the vague stirrings of sexual desire I'd been feeling suddenly focused themselves in the form of a rapid fluttering between my legs.

We got back on our marks. I felt a real sense of fear and excitement. I was going to kiss my best friend. On camera. As the bodies in front of us began to writhe and moan, my confidence grew. They didn't have any problem with simulating full sex with multiple partners! Why should I be nervous about a little kiss between friends?

We heard Darrel's cue.

'Jade, Tania, *go*,' he said from somewhere behind the camera.

Tania and I looked into each other's eyes and then I closed mine. The next thing I felt was sweet hot breath on my lips and then her mouth closing in on mine. She tasted of the apple juice we'd been drinking, sweet and fizzy, and I hoped I did too. I kissed her back, softly at first, and was surprised by how warm and silky she felt. Intuitively, I slid my tongue ever so lightly in between Tania's lips, hoping she wouldn't reject it. But she received my tongue greedily, parted her lips wide, extended her own tongue to meet mine.

Our bodies moved together. The fabric of our clothes was so sheer, I could feel her hardening nipples as our breasts rubbed together. She was throbbing with the same heat and the energy I felt. I placed one hand on Tania's arse and pulled her hips towards mine. She pushed herself close. My mind was racing: I was fluctuating between letting my body tell me what felt good and thinking, this is *Tania!* What am I doing? One thing was for sure: I was no longer relying on looking at the bodies on the sofa to get horny. All I was thinking about, all I was feeling, all I could picture, was Tania.

The dark, sticky gloss that we both wore smeared all over our lips as we kissed more urgently and passionately. Then abruptly the spell was broken.

'Cut!' Darrel's voice broke my reverie. Tania and I pulled apart, at first shy to meet each other's eyes because now the camera was off us, did we have to pretend that that moment of hot electricity hadn't been real?

'Jade, what the fuck? I didn't know you could kiss like that,' said Tania, and she was only half joking. Her face – and I guess mine, too – was smeared with the glaze of the dark burgundy lipstick, like we'd been eating crushed berries or dark, syrupy wine.

'Tidy them up, but not too much,' said Darrel to the make-up girl. 'I like the idea that they've just come from, I don't know, a hot sex session or something. That they were kissing before they even saw the orgy.' And then to us, 'You girls okay with that? You're naturals on camera. Which is just as well, as we've got to shoot that whole scene again – without your leg obscuring Jenny's breasts, this time, please Oliver,' he said, addressing a naked man who lay face down on one of the fan dancers.

'Righto,' said Oliver, clearly unfazed by the whole thing. Clearly Tania and I were the only ones not treating this whole experience with professional detachment.

We shot the scene again, and this time as Tania and I gazed at the actors faking sex before us, we did it for show, both knowing we wanted to get back to kissing each other. This time there was no hesitation and we went straight in for the kiss, our lips finding each other automatically, the length of our bodies pressed together. Tania slid her knee between my two so that that the top of her leg was pressed between mine, the top of her thigh just brushing the sensitive area between my legs. The silver fox-fur stole around my neck slid off my shoulders and fell to the ground, stroking my body as it tumbled.

In the background I was dimly aware of Darrel shouting instructions. 'Okay guys! That's great! Really go for it. Improvise! Do what feels good!'

Improvising, I took a saucer of 'champagne' and put it to Tania's lips. She took a sip, then a greedy gulp, and lurched back at me, kissing me and transferring the sweet, sparkling liquid from her mouth to mine. The juice ran down my neck and on to my clavicle bone. On impulse, Tania put her lips to my neck like a vampire. She licked up the liquid, her tongue and teeth sucking greedily at my skin.

I looked down at the smooth, pale nape of her neck and the crown of golden curls on her head. I could see the main action still going on: the camera crew were focusing on the ten half-naked bodies. Two girls dressed as fan dancers were kneeling opposite each other now, sequins peeling away from their nipples and falling on to their companions as the women kissed passionately, tits and tongues searching for each other. I envied them their semi-clothed state and wished that Tania and I were on a bed, without all these clothes to stop us from the skin-on-skin action I craved. Her breath was on my upper breast now, and my nipple grew harder, upright, begging for her lips and teeth on it.

'This is great,' said Darrel, rubbing his hands together. 'I'm just gonna let the camera run until everyone's out of ideas.'

I reached for a bunch of grapes that lay on the banqueting table. I held it aloft, feeling like an ancient Roman goddess. Lowering the grapes, I held them between my lips and Tania's. The pair of us fought for the fruit greedily, devouring the grapes, our tongues clashing. We did to the grapes what we wanted to do to each other's tits, sucking and biting voraciously. When we kissed this time, Tania tasted sweet and our faces were glazed with the juice of the fruit. My hand ran to Tania's nipple, erect and proud through her gown and my fingertip swirled small circles around the soft flesh surrounding it. Her kisses grew deeper in response, so I increased the pressure, my fingernail lightly scratching that most sensitive area. Tania let out an involuntary moan of pleasure and at that sound, I felt my pussy grow wet.

'Cut!' came Darrel's voice. 'That's great work, guys. I don't think we need to do another take. I've got everything I need right there. That's a wrap! Shoot over!'

I was torn between disappointment that it was over so quickly and relief that I could shake off these uncharacteristic feelings of lust for Tania and return to normal now I didn't have to kiss her on camera. Just five more minutes of filming, and who knows how far I would have gone?

'Okay,' continued Darrel. 'Thanks guys. That's great. Everyone get cleaned up and I'll see you in the bar next door in an hour or so. I can't promise real champagne but I will buy you all a drink if you get there quick enough.'

The lure of free booze meant that everyone rushed to the dressing rooms – which were actually the toilets – to change back into their own clothes. Tania and I followed, holding hands.

We'd held hands, linked arms, hugged in the past, in a close girly, chummy way, but this time, we didn't speak, and she caressed the soft skin on the inside of my wrist, in a way she'd never done before.

The dressing room was packed with laughing drama students. If anyone was surprised by what we'd just done, they didn't mention it. I reached for the cold cream to remove my make-up. 'Don't,' said Tania. 'I like you looking like that.'

'What?' I said, suddenly shy.

'I like the person you are in those clothes, that hair, that make-up. And because of what I want to do to you, I need you to remain in character.'

'What do you want to do to me?' I said, although I already knew.

And she took my hand and led me into a large washroom cubicle. Like the main restaurant, it was also decorated in period style with palms and oak panelling. We looked at ourselves in a mirror: it was us, but it wasn't. The clothes, hair and make-up had transformed us into decadent women from another era, hungry for the next sensation.

'Oh, Jade,' said Tania. 'I need to finish what we started on camera.'

We undressed each other. Tania simply held her arms up and I pulled her gown over her head. I stepped out of my own dress. My boobs were much smaller than Tania's full, round tits, but my nipples were so hard that my whole breasts almost doubled in size. Tania's nipples were nut-brown, dark and erect, her ample chest rising and falling as her breathing quickened.

We leant in for another kiss, bodies colliding, skin on skin at last. It was so much more raw and sexual than it had been when we'd performed in costume before the camera. This time nothing was for show: it was all about how it felt. Tania's breasts clashing with mine so hard that they were squashed flat against my own tits was an amazing sensation. My bush rubbed against hers, creating a crackle of static electricity.

Then she did what I'd needed her to do in front of the camera and bent down and put her lips to my nipple, sucking and swirling so softly that I couldn't believe I'd gone my whole life without ever feeling something so amazing and sensual. I caressed the sensitive skin on her neck, whispered into her ear, 'Jesus, Tania, I can't believe we're doing this but it feels so good . . .'

Tania fastened her teeth over my tit and bit down, gently but enough to make me cry out.

'My turn now,' she said, offering me a large, round breast: I wrapped my lips around the nipple, sucking it softly at first but getting greedy as I got carried away: I wanted to taste her whole tit in my mouth, and spread my lips as wide as they could, trying to cram the whole bulbous breast inside my mouth.

While I was doing this, Tania's fingers found my clitoris and began to rub it, softly and gently, making me moan into her breast. I pulled my head up from her tit and kissed her, a deep, probing kiss, then pulled away to look at her one more time: feasting my eyes on her between kisses re-ignited my desire for her.

Tania's legs were apart and she was staggering, dizzy with lust, her back against the cold tiles of the wall. We'd had enough conversations about men for me to know that she liked her partners to be dominant, take charge of her in bed. Unfulfilled lust made me aggressive and confident and I knew I could give her the forcefulness she needed. I didn't need to work on her clit: she was already dripping.

The smell, a sweet nutty odour like the one I sniffed in my own panties when I was aroused, was an aromatic, spicy perfume that filled the air and made my pulse pound harder and faster than it ever had before. I pulled my fingers together and thrust all five of them inside her. When she whimpered I made my other hand into a fist and stuffed it into her mouth.

She bit down hard, my hand muffling her moans of pleasure. I twisted my fingers around inside her cunt, feeling the little raised knob of flesh that was her G-spot, and used my knuckle to stimulate it, slowly moving up and down, up and down until her moans became screams of ecstasy.

Tania was so caught up in what I was doing to her that she stopped stroking my clitoris. Desire made me greedy and selfish: I fisted Tania harder and faster, willing her climax to come so that she could give me mine. When she eventually had an orgasm, she bit down on one of my hands and the muscles of her pussy convulsed around the other.

I had never needed to come so bad in my whole life. I pulled my hand out of Tania: it was glossy with her juices. I took that slippery hand and grabbed hers: she knew what she had to do. Her legs gave way beneath her and she slumped to the floor. I stood over her, my pussy at her eye level. She put two fingers inside me and then slowly drew them partway out, then in again: she licked my pussy lips and then held the tip of her tongue against my clitoris, stiff, wet and slowly circling the bud. My clit began to thrum hard, my climax building inside my body. Tania stopped licking abruptly and then sucked *hard* on my clit. With a little flick of her tongue, I came, knees shaking like never before, the tension releasing itself and robbing me of control over my own body. I collapsed, sliding my pussy down the whole length of Tania's body, until I was sitting opposite her on the bathroom floor. We had one more kiss: I tasted myself on her tongue.

On the other side of the mahogany door we could hear the other cast members flouncing and giggling and Darrel's voice going, 'Where's Jade and Tania? They better not have gone home with those dresses.' We looked at each other and got the giggles – insane laughter that had us clutching at each other anew. I knew what we were both thinking: if only he'd been in there with us, he'd have got some footage for his film that would have made the orgy scene seem positively tame by comparison.

After we'd untangled each other's coiffures and wiped away the make-up, we were just Jade and Tania again: the adventure we'd had seemed like a fantasy a million miles away from anything we'd ever do again. I don't know what came over us: it was the clothes, the make-up, the feeling of being another woman from a decadent era with a licence to do whatever we wanted: for that magic afternoon, reality was suspended.

I look at Tania now, with her messy hair and fresh face, and she seems like a different person to the old-time seductress who made me come hard in a restaurant bathroom. I guess that sometimes it's only when we tap into fantasy that reality feels so good.

FOURPLAY

Could you imagine watching your man making love to someone else? Think carefully before you answer. Most of us are a little possessive, a little jealous when it comes to our men: the thought of seeing him with another woman is enough to make us want to tie him to the bed so he doesn't get the chance! But a surprising number of women get off on the idea of their guy fucking other women, actively seeking out those very circumstances .

Jessica, the woman who shared the following story with me, never thought she would be able to handle it. But one blistering night on an island far from home, she found that the opposite was true . . .

I live for the sex I have on holiday. Nothing else touches it. For most of the year, Alex and I have our little routine: a lazy lie in on a Sunday morning that turns into sex in one of our two favourite positions, sweet and loving and over in exactly twenty-one minutes. But on holiday . . . oh, it's very different. Once we're sipping cocktails on some tropical beach, the lust kicks in and within hours of landing at the airport, we're fucking like a pair of teenagers who've just discovered sex rather than the old married couple we really are. I say old: we're not even thirty yet, but when you've been together for seven years, things inevitably slow down, get a little samey. But even when sex feels stuck in a rut, I don't whinge and I don't worry. I just book a holiday because I know that as soon as we get some sea, sunshine and sand in our systems, sizzling sex always follows.

This holiday I'm talking about was the most lavish we'd ever been on: it was a tiny, exclusive Seychelles resort, an all-inclusive complex with no annoying kids, endless free cocktails, unlimited gorgeous food and powdery white sandy beaches bathed in all the rays we could soak up. And our accommodation was a private cabin on stilts, jutting out into a lotus pond. A huge white bed, scattered with exotic petals dominated the cabin. We arrived, jet-lagged and exhausted, and fell asleep to the sound of the water lapping at the walls. When we awoke, late in the afternoon, we were feeling hot, in both senses of the word. I looked at Alex's body. I still find it as beautiful as I did seven years ago, more so; I love his flat stomach, his powerful legs and the line of black hair that starts below his navel and squiggles down to his dick. As I watched his cock, it began to swell: I stroked it until it was rock-hard while his hand found my clitoris and began to caress it the way he knew I loved. We slipped into the kind of slow, leisurely love-making you enjoy when you've got nowhere to go and no one to think about except each other. The holiday was off to a good start.

That evening, we slipped on light clothes and explored the resort. It was highly sensual, with bright flowers scenting the air and vivid fabrics hanging up at every window and draped over every surface. Any one of the resort's staff could have carved out a career as a professional model: as well as being enticing eye candy, they were fun, friendly and did everything they could to make us feel comfortable.

Because it was such an expensive resort, the other couples were just as glamorous, young and good-looking. As I followed my handsome husband up a wooden path towards a fairy-lit outdoor restaurant, a few heads turned get an eyeful of him. I felt a stab of jealousy followed by pride that such a good-looking guy was with me and an undercurrent of something else, an unexpected frisson of desire that made me slide my hand down the front of his top and give his nipple a playful tweak. He bent down and bit my hand, making me giggle.

There were no free tables but the waiter suggested we take a place at the bar with a drink while we waited. I had no objection to being served cocktails by a barman who looked like an Adonis, so over we went, sliding on to two stools next to an impossibly blond and tanned couple, both dressed head-to-toe in white. Trying to get comfortable on my seat, I inadvertently elbowed the man's colourful cocktail across the bar and on to his white shirt. An orange stain sank into the crisp cotton, making it transparent: I could make out each ripple of his six-pack and see that his nipples were pale brown. For a few seconds, I was so absorbed by this that I forgot to apologise.

'I'm so sorry!' I said, remembering my manners. 'Let me get you another drink! Let me buy you another *shirt*! Oh dear.'

'No worries,' he said, in a broad, sexy, Australian twang, and then introduced himself. 'I'm Brad, and this is my missus, Laura. Excuse me one moment.' He unbuttoned his top revealing a ripped, golden-brown body.

'Hi Laura, Brad,' I said, shaking the tanned hands that were extended to me and trying not to be distracted by the topless man, 'I'm Jessica and this is Alex.'

'You're Brits, right? You're looking a bit pale. Just got here?'

I nodded, as Alex got the drinks in, telling the barman to refill Brad's glass and get Laura another drink, too. 'That's right,' I said. 'Isn't it beautiful?'

'Oh, it is,' agreed Laura, her hands resting lightly

across Brad's chest. 'We've been here ten days – only got a few more days to go, haven't we, baby?'

Brad and Laura were the most demonstrative couple I'd ever met. Alex and I could be prone to public displays of affection, and had often been told to 'get a room' by friends, but we were the epitome of English reserve compared to this couple. Their legs were entwined, and their hands were all over each other, constantly stroking. At one point, Brad slid his hand under the spaghetti strap of Laura's sundress, caressing her collarbone and I inadvertently caught a glimpse of her breast, as tanned as the rest of her, and a pale pink nipple.

After a while our waiter came back. 'I'm sorry you've been waiting so long,' he said.

'Not at all,' said Alex. 'We've had a good time here at the bar.' And it was true – although the cocktails on an empty stomach were something I'd regret the next day, right now they'd loosened us all up and made us enjoy our time together.

'Ah,' said the waiter. 'You see, we have one table for four but none for two. If you and your friends would like to eat together . . .'

We all looked at each other. 'Sure, why not?' said Laura, and Brad jokingly added, 'We want to stay as near as possible to you guys, anyway. You're so bloody pasty, you make our tans look shit hot!'

Over a dinner of seafood and salad under the stars, the four of us talked as though we'd been friends for ages. I couldn't remember when I'd last had such fun. The atmosphere was definitely flirty – once or twice Brad brushed against me or laid a hand on my arm when he was making a point, and I saw Laura push her elbows together so that her tits looked bigger when Alex was looking, but I didn't mind. It was kind of safe, flirting within a secure relationship. It's not like anything would ever come of it . . . would it?

As the plates were cleared away, talk turned, as it does when you're pissed, to sex. Laura leaned forward and said in a conspiratorial whisper, 'There are some amazing secluded beaches around here where you can, you know, have a little couple time. We found a cove yesterday that you swim around to and there's no one there. You can just lie down and make love with the sun on your back. Have you ever done that?' I shook my head, excited by the image I had of Brad and Laura making love in the sand. 'Oh, you must,' she continued. 'Sunbathing and fucking at the same time – what's not to like?'

And of course, we then had to upstage each other with tales of our most daring erotic adventures. Alex and I told Brad and Laura about the time our car had broken down on the motorway, and we'd been caught fucking in the back seat by the AA man: they came back with a story about a sex club they'd been to for a laugh and Laura had ended up giving Brad head on the stage. We then told a story about our honeymoon when I'd given Alex a handjob on a hotel balcony and he'd come quicker than he expected and shot a load of spunk on to some sunbathers below. The four of us were laughing hysterically at that one when Brad and Laura dropped their bombshell.

They exchanged a private glance and she said, 'And then of course there was the time we had that foursome.'

'Ah yeah!' said Brad wistfully. 'Beautiful, good-looking couple that we met at a party and took home. They looked a bit like you guys, actually. Yeah, that was a wild night.'

'Have you ever . . . ?' began Laura.

'No, no,' said Alex before I could reply for us. 'We've never done anything like that.'

As he spoke, my mind went into overdrive, flashing images of me and Brad fucking, sending a strong message to my clitoris, which started to throb. I couldn't believe I was reacting like this: I'm normally the faithful – even jealous – type, yet here I was fantasising about hot sex with a man who wasn't my husband – and feeling hornier than I had in a long, long time.

'But I'd never say never!' I chipped in, and I saw Alex next to me shoot a sharp, but not cross, look in my direction that said, 'We'll talk about this later!'

'I like people who'll try anything once,' said Brad. 'I, on the other hand, prefer to try things twice.' And under the table, he ran a bare foot up the length of my shin. It was the first time in seven years that I'd had skin-on-skin contact like this with a man other than Alex, and the effect of Brad's flesh touching mine was powerful, my throbbing clit expanding, intensifying, demanding satisfaction.

As the waiter came to tell us the bar was closing, Brad whipped his foot away, leaving me confused and massively turned on. The atmosphere was suddenly a little awkward and formal again. Maybe Brad sensed he'd gone a little too far.

'So . . .' said Laura. 'We should do this again. See you guys tomorrow?'

'Yes!' said Alex and I in unison. We waved goodbye to the Aussie couple, and made our way back to our cabin along a little wooden jetty lit with tiny candles.

'I think we've just had what they call an indecent proposal,' Alex was giggling, a sure sign that he was nervous.

'Not exactly the most obvious place you'd expect to meet a pair of swingers,' I said, and then, 'But if we were going to, we couldn't choose a better couple, don't you think?'

'Are you thinking what I'm thinking?'

'Well . . .' said Alex, as he opened the door to our cabin. 'I was looking at your tits in that top, and I was thinking how proud I am of you, and how it's almost a shame that no one else gets to enjoy them.'

'Mm,' I murmured, picking up Alex's thread, 'And I was noticing the hard-on you got watching Laura's tits and imagining your dick inside her. I thought it would freak me out, but actually, it was kind of hot . . .'

Alex and I were getting closer and closer, drawing in each other's breath as we swapped fantasies. The thought of us swapping partners was something we'd never discussed before but now that the subject had come up, it was clear that it was turning us both on. I felt my wetness seep on to my inner thigh: Alex's dick, harder than usual, prodded my lower belly.

Then we were on each other, devouring voraciously, teeth and lips clashing. I pulled Alex's shorts down over his hips, freeing his hard-on, while he yanked my panties to one side and threw me back on the bed. He was inside me immediately, spearing me with his hard-on fatter and harder than I'd known it in years. Within seconds I came around his dick by just the pounding of his rock-solid cock filling my pussy. My orgasm was over all too soon, and while my pussy was still twitching, I grabbed Alex's arse with both hands, pulled him in even deeper so that he came, spurting his juices into my insides. We lay on the bed, tangled up in each other, struggling for breath, exhilarated by what we'd just done.

'And that was only thinking about it,' I said. 'Imagine how charged we'd feel actually *doing* it.'

'You horny little bitch, Jess,' said Alex, as we made our way to the outside shower to wash sweat and spunk off our bodies. 'Seven years together and you're still finding new ways to get me off. I knew I did the right thing marrying you.'

❧

The next morning we awoke hungover and giggly. 'Do you remember what we talked about last night?' said Alex.

'I do . . . it was horny at the time, but would you ever have the balls to go ahead with it? I mean, do you really think we could handle seeing each other fucking somebody else?'

Alex was reflective. 'I think because we talked about it, it'll be fine. Just remember how wet it made you last night,' and to make his point, he slid his finger into my pussy and then licked it. 'You're soaking now just thinking about it,' he said, and the thin white sheet betrayed his erection beneath.

'You're right,' I said, and reached for his dick, hoping for a repeat performance.

'No,' said Alex, brushing away my hand as it closed around his smooth, hard penis. 'If we're going to do this, let's save ourselves for later. Delayed gratification, darling. We can make the foreplay last all day . . .'

'Clever, aren't you?' I said. 'I knew I did the right thing marrying you.'

❧

We had breakfast on the veranda of our cabin, so we didn't see Brad and Laura until later that morning. But in this small, exclusive resort, there wasn't much chance of avoiding each other for too long. When we went for a pre-lunch swim on the private beach, they were already there: Laura was topless and Brad wore a pair of baggy surfer's shorts that showed off that built-up torso, flat stomach and strong, muscular legs.

'That's not fair!' I pointed out to Alex. 'You get to see everything she's got to offer, but his bod is left up to my imagination.'

We stood under a palm tree, transfixed as Brad oiled Laura's back with suntan lotion and then turned over to massage it into her breasts. She looked up and saw us, and broke into a smile that showed off her white teeth.

'Hey guys,' said Laura, waving at us so that her round, high breasts bounced in the sun. 'Come and join us.'

We made small talk, not mentioning the foursome we'd talked about the night before. The atmosphere was definitely charged anyway without continuing the further tales of our past sexual exploits. From behind my sunglasses, I kept sneaking glances at Brad. He was beautifully bronzed, with messy blond curls and blue eyes that crinkled when he smiled: every teenage girl's surfer fantasy. Once or twice, I saw him looking at my body, paler and slimmer than Laura's athletic, tanned figure. A bulge in his shorts told me he liked what he saw, too.

When he offered to rub lotion into my back, I said yes, knowing that Alex wouldn't mind. I was right: he offered to do Laura's at the same time. Brad's hands were larger than Alex's, and rougher, but his touch was lighter, subtler than my husband's. I was gratified to feel, fleetingly, Brad's erection sticking into my back.

He flipped me over to do my front and without asking began to rub oily lotion into my breasts, hands smooth, brushing lightly over my nipples which grew erect under his fingers. I turned my head and saw Alex doing the same to Laura: his pale biscuit skin made a beautiful contrast with her sun-baked Bondi Beach complexion. Alex's touch was firmer: I saw his fingers dig into her tits, which sprang back as he massaged them. He moved his attentions – and his hands – lower down her midriff, past her navel . . . he was going dangerously close to Laura's bikini line, and her closed eyes and the way she arched her back were a clear indication that she was loving every sensation. I couldn't take my eyes off them. It was hot as hell – like a porno film that you could smell, hear and, if you reached out just a few inches, touch, as well. If this was a taste of what we could expect tonight, I couldn't wait till sunset.

When the guys finished massaging us girls, Brad made an announcement: 'Listen, we're off to get some lunch now, but why don't we hook up again this evening?'

'I'd love that,' said Alex and I simultaneously.

'Cool,' said Laura. 'Well, we can order drinks and dinner for four to eat on our terrace if you like. It's so lovely overlooking the lotus pond, and we won't be disturbed by *anyone*.' The subtext of her words was unmistakable. Tonight, she meant, we will have perfect privacy.

'We'll look forward to it,' said Alex. We watched Brad and Laura walk back to their cabin, their arms wrapped around each other's waists and their oiled, beautiful bodies glistening in the scorching sunlight.

'Well, Jess,' said Alex, leaning in to nibble my ear, 'I think we've got ourselves a rendezvous.'

❧

We dressed that night as carefully as though for a first date, which in a way it was. Alex wore a light cotton shirt unbuttoned to the navel, which showed off his toned chest and the beginnings of a tan, with a pair of loose, khaki trousers. He looked chic and elegant. I wore a blue silk dress: I deliberated for ages about whether to bother with underwear. In the end I went bra-less – for the feel-good factor as well as the look-good one – and slipped on a pair of black lace knickers that tied at the sides. Alex only had to glimpse this pair to want to get me out of them so I hoped they'd have the same effect on Brad. Finally, I slipped my feet into jewelled sandals that made my legs go on forever. A spritz of perfume, a couple of condoms in Alex's pocket and we were ready to go.

We arrived at Brad and Laura's cabin at seven thirty as agreed. Before we knocked on the door, Alex pulled me to him and kissed me, slow and wet and deep and just a little aggressive.

'If you feel freaked out at any point, we can always back out,' he said. 'Okay?'

I didn't answer, but took his hands in mine. I placed one on an erect nipple, and another I slid into my panties which were already damp. If anything, I was even more up for this than Alex.

Dinner was lobster, washed down with champagne – but we drank sparingly, the adrenaline and lust a natural high that no alcohol could match. Brad was topless, which was wildly distracting, wearing only a pair of combat trousers, a small, shiny conch pendant on a leather thong around his neck.

I sat between Brad and Alex, and opposite Laura. Brad fed me bits of lobster and held a glass of champagne to my lips. 'Taste it,' he said, 'It's really good.'

If Alex and I were wondering about how to make the first move, we needn't have: Brad and Laura's previous experience meant they knew how to take control of the situation. Brad walked his hand up the inside of my thigh. At the same time, I noticed Laura's fingers creeping round the small of Alex's back, making small massaging movements. When she slipped her slender brown fingers down the waistband of his shorts, Alex's pupils dilated and his whole body relaxed under her touch.

I parted my legs to show Brad that this was all cool, that I wanted this. After that, things started to happen. Brad leaned in to kiss me over the table, tasting of seafood and champagne. The dark blond stubble on his chin made him feel very different to Alex, who was always clean shaven. Brad's skin was harsh, yet his kiss was softer and slower than I was used to. This delicate, leisurely style of kissing made a thrilling change from Alex's hard, probing style.

Alex was on Laura, devouring her: she lunging at him, obviously getting off on my husband's powerful, forceful kisses.

All four of us came up for air at the same time.

'So,' said Laura, 'Shall we take this inside?' she led Alex by the hand to the edge of the bed: his hands were all over her, tearing at her clothes. Like me, she wore only a simple sundress. Alex ripped it off her with one move: she stood there, naked and reached for my husband, ripping the buttons of his white shirt while he kicked off his shoes and slid his trousers down over his hips. His tan lines were clearly defined now: his white butt cheeks were like two moons, and the flesh of his twitching dick was highlighted against her tanned stomach as they moved together and kissed. I stood transfixed as my fantasy came to life in front of me: I knew exactly how it felt to be worked on by Alex, how his rough passion awakened the same kind of response in me, and putting myself in Laura's position really helped me to get off. The pang between my legs turned into an ache of arousal.

Laura drew away from Alex's embrace, her breath coming in short, wild rasps: his hands felt for her tits, pulling them out as far as they'd go and then dropping them suddenly: all of us watched as they bounced and fell. 'I want to taste you, Alex,' said Laura in her Aussie accent and knelt down before him. She gazed at his twitching hard-on, admiring the creamy skin and the thick vein that pulsed along the underside of his cock before licking her lips and slowly easing him into her mouth. The look on Alex's face was of pure pleasure: I knew how much he loved to get head, and Laura clearly loved giving it.

Brad had been standing behind me the whole time, cock rock-hard and pressing into the small of my back. He smelled of coconut oil and sex. He pushed further into my back, kissed the sensitive skin at the nape of my neck, slid his hands up underneath my sundress, found my lace panties.

'Oh, that's nice,' he said, undoing first one side of my panties. His soft, rough finger pressed gently on to my swollen clitoris, making me cry out. 'Oh, Jess,' he sighed into my neck. 'You've got a very welcoming pussy. Very nice indeed.'

Sucking and nuzzling my shoulder, Brad worked on my clitoris, rubbing gently and softly, as he delicately unlaced the other side of my knickers. He then pulled them through my legs, taking the ribbons and tickling my lips with them in a back-and-forth motion before putting them to his nose and inhaling deeply. 'I can tell how horny you are by just how good these smell,' and he made me breathe my own scent in too.

It was true, they were evidence of the raging desire that had welled up within me and spilled out into my panties. He let the underwear go and undid the strap that held my halterneck dress in place. It fell to the floor in a puddle around me. He took off his shorts: we were both naked now, the cold of his shell necklace pressing into my back. I kept my sandals on so that we remained the same height. He reached for my breasts, cupped them, curled a rough dry thumb around each nipple. All the while we watched Alex and Laura, joined at the lip and dick, putting on a live, exclusive and very hot sex show.

Alex and Laura changed places and stumbled back on to the bed. He fell back and Laura worked her way up his body with kisses before jumping on top and straddling him. Alex liked to be on top with me, and was clearly enjoying the surrender of having someone take charge of him. She took a condom from its wrapper on her bedside table, put the tip in her mouth, and smoothed it onto Alex's pulsing dick.

She gave him a final few seconds of oral pleasure before spreading her legs over his cock. Mercilessly, she grabbed his hard-on with a firm hand, forced it into her neat-looking, hungry slit. I could see his dick going in and out, disappearing and then reappearing, on and on, in and out. Her energy was boundless. 'Touch my clit,' she said. Alex obeyed instantly. It wasn't my style to boss him around like this, but it was so thrilling watching another woman play the dominatrix with him.

Brad turned me around to kiss me, and for a moment I closed my eyes, let my body melt under his soft, sensual lips. As beautiful as the moment was, I didn't want to miss a second of Alex and Laura. 'I want you inside me,' I said to Brad. 'But I need to see them fucking, too.'

Brad nodded. 'God, they look horny as hell, don't they?' he said. 'I don't know what's making me harder – the way they look or the way you feel.'

I turned to face the bed again. I heard a wrapper

tearing as Brad prepared to put on a condom and the snap as he rolled it on to his penis. He thrust a knee between my legs, parted my thighs, held my waist with a strong brown arm and then, with a force that took my breath away, penetrated me. His dick wasn't as fat as Alex's, but it was longer. The ribbed condom provided extra friction as he thrust in and out of me with smooth, slow thrusts that echoed his gentle, leisurely kisses. His balls were slapping against the top of my thighs. I could feel that his cock and balls were shaved and I thought about how I would like to give Alex an extra intimate haircut later: God, what a horny image. My arousal was turned up a notch.

I wasn't used to being fucked standing up: the spreading pleasure that came from inside my pussy was brand new to me: hotter, wider, less pulsating than usual. As I adjusted to this new, intense kind of pleasure, I realised that Brad had found my elusive G-spot. He continued to play with my clitoris and fondle my breasts at the same time, building up a wave of pleasure that was only intensified by the scene in front of me, Laura riding Alex like a cowgirl at a rodeo.

'God, you're so tight,' said Brad into my shoulder. 'I'm warning you, I'm gonna come soon. But I'm gonna get you there first.' I didn't doubt it, and as he rolled my clit between his thumb and forefinger, I felt the heat rise to my cheeks and chest, a sure sign that an orgasm was only seconds away.

Right then, Alex closed his eyes. I knew this meant he was about to come: Laura must have sensed it too, because she parted the top of her pussy lips to expose her clit and started to rub it, harder and faster than I'd ever touched myself. Her orgasm hit seconds before Alex's did: she remained deadly silent while her body surrendered to the convulsions, her brown breasts seeming to lift and swell, beads of sweat rolling down those tits and between her shoulder blades. She was still rocking back and forth when Alex let out a roar of pleasure and his hips pumped into her pussy once, twice, three times before he sank, spent, back on to the pillows. He opened his eyes, looked briefly at Laura, gave her a sleepy smile and then turned his full attention to Brad and me.

Now it was our turn to put on a performance. Brad maintained the regular, pounding rhythm of his thrusts and kept circling my clit. But it was Alex who made me come, his eyes feasting on me, loving what he saw, licking his lips and moaning with pleasure and pride. The fire in my cheeks burned hot and intense as I came, my pussy clutching at Brad's cock with an intensity I'd never known before, forcing him to climax, too. My legs turned to quicksilver beneath me, and if it hadn't been for Brad's brawny, steadying arm, I'd have collapsed on the floor. As it was, we just managed to stagger to the bed, where the four of us lay, stroking and caressing each other, taking a few moments to come back down to earth.

After washing our bodies clean in the outdoor showers, we said our goodbyes – Laura and I hugged, and Brad and I indulged in a last lingering kiss while Laura and Alex enjoyed a final grapple. She ended by giving a playful squeeze to his still-sensitive dick to show him who was boss. By the time Alex and I walked back to our own cabin, the dawn was beginning to break over the lush resort, casting an unreal pink light over the landscape and a hazy mist over the events of the evening. We still couldn't quite believe we'd really done it.

Brad and Laura flew home the next morning. I was happy about that: last night had been so wild and intense, I wasn't sure I wanted to see them again and make boring small talk over coffee. I wanted to leave the night of lived-out fantasy intact, perfect. For the next few days, Alex and I only left the bedroom to swim and eat. Our experience had made us closer than ever: I'd call it a second honeymoon, only it was even more horny and intense than our first. Then we actually talked about doing it again one day, but when the time was right.

The night before we were due to leave, we had drinks at the bar. We found ourselves sitting next to a good-looking couple, pale and just off the flight, about our own age. Something about the way the guy was looking at me made me nudge my husband and point them out.

'Hey,' said Alex. 'I'm Alex, and this is my wife Jessica. Are you guys new here? Let us show you around . . .'

THE SINNER

What is it about forbidden fruit that makes it taste so sweet? It's an unwritten rule that the more unobtainable a man is, the more attractive he'll appear.

The woman who told me the following confession is an accomplished journalist in her thirties, a beautiful and successful woman who thrives on a challenge, especially when it comes to men.

But then she met the ultimate unavailable man. In this story, her rival isn't another woman, but a whole belief system and way of life. She resisted for as long as she could. And in the end, it wasn't her willpower that gave out.

How would you have behaved in her position?

My job as a roving reporter takes me to all sorts of odd places, but none as remote as an isolated farmhouse in Wales last October. I drove there from London, my little city car struggling with the rough terrain of winding rural roads, to interview a farmer about the highly unexciting subject of government subsidies. By the time I'd finished talking to him, written up the article and emailed the whole thing over to the newsdesk, night had already begun to fall. The autumn skies looked dark and gloomy.

'I think a storm's on its way,' said the farmer. 'Are you sure you want to drive home in this weather? These roads can be quite treacherous.'

'I'll be fine,' I said. 'Thank you.' Charming as the farmer had been, I didn't relish the idea of sleeping in a Welsh farmhouse. I'd had enough countryside for one day, thank you very much.

But I should have listened to him: I'd been in the car for half an hour when the rain started. Within five minutes, I could barely see the road and my tyres struggled to grip the tarmac. My sports car was hopelessly out of depth with the puddles and potholes, and I should have hardly been surprised when I veered off the road and my back wheels became stuck in a muddy ditch. I pulled out my mobile to call the recovery service, but my battery was dead. Now fear began to replace frustration. There was no way I could stay here in my sinking, waterlogged car.

I had to think fast. About half a mile up a steep hill, I saw a light. I decided to go for it. I soon discovered, however, that a lifetime of aerobics classes had done little to equip me for fell-walking in the rain with only a tiny torch to illuminate my way. It took nearly two hours to reach my destination. By the time I'd climbed the top of the hill to be met by wrought iron gates in front of a large, dark, brick building, I was freezing, soaked and fighting back tears of exhaustion. This was no farmhouse, or holiday cottage – there was an old-fashioned bell pull on a rope in front of an imposing wooden door, and candles flickering in sconces. I pulled on the bell-rope and soon saw a figure in a long raincoat coming to rescue me.

As the figure drew nearer I saw that it was a stout, middle-aged man and that he wore not a raincoat but a monk's habit, shabby brown fabric and a hood shielding him from the rain. He looked astonished to see me, but his face softened when I began to cry, with relief as much as anything else.

'Oh, dear. You poor creature,' he said. 'Come in, come on in. Don't worry. You're safe now,' and he led me through the door of the huge, gothic building. I found myself, soaking and shivering, in a candlelit hall, with arched doors leading to long, dim corridors. Five or six other men, all dressed like my rescuer, hovered nervously in the doorways.

'The first thing to do is to get you out of those wet clothes. There's a chamber in there; dry yourself and we'll fetch you a robe. Oh, thank you,' he said, as a figure handed him a light-brown hooded cloak, exactly like the one they all wore. 'I'm sorry,' he said with a shy smile. 'You're actually the first female visitor the monastery has had for nearly ten years, so we don't have anything more suitable. But we'll get your own things dry as soon as we can.'

'Brother Michael!' he called. 'Please show the young lady to a chamber.' At this, a tall, rangy youth stepped out of the shadows. He couldn't have been much older than twenty: he had a shy, graceless beauty that I'd never seen in a man before. His short hair was strawberry blond and worn in a Caesar crop. His skin was freckled, his blue eyes piercing and he had a square-jawed, classically handsome face and full, pink lips. If you were a man in a bar in London, and not an inmate of a monastery in Wales, I'd be all over you in a minute, I thought, then immediately felt guilty.

Inside the little room, I dried myself with a rough, meagre towel and wrapped myself in my monk's habit, leaving my clothes in a neat pile. I felt peculiar at the thought of some celibate monk touching my expensive red lingerie. The robe was far too big, and scratchy because I was naked beneath. Normally, I'd have found the notion of a layer of wool between my naked body and a building full of sex-starved men something of a thrill. Today, I was too tired even to be horny and just wanted to sleep. The young monk, Brother Michael, led me through labyrinthine corridors to a small room with a bed, basin and a toilet. A small fire burned in the grate: my last memory is of shrugging off the shroud and slipping, naked but very warm, in between the fur rugs on the bed, exhausted by my day.

The dawn light woke me, streaming through the uncurtained window, shining on my naked breasts. My first instinct was to draw the blankets up to cover myself and my second was 'Oh God – whose bed am I in?' When I wake up naked in a strange place it's generally a sign I'd had sex the night before. But as I looked around the plain, sandstone room it all came back to me: Wales, the interview, the storm, the wheelspin, the exhausting walk up the hill in the rain, the kind men who had taken me in for the night.

I looked out of the window. The sun hid behind grey clouds in a white sky. With my phone dead and no watch, I didn't know what time it was. There were distant signs of life: I could hear footsteps and, far away, doors opening and closing and the sound of voices chanting.

A knock on the door brought me to my senses and I sat bolt upright in bed. With no time to dress, I wrapped myself in the fur rugs, walked over and opened the door. Brother Michael was crouching over a tray with water, bread and fruit on it, his eyes level with my exposed knees. I could feel his breath on my legs.

'Hello,' I said. 'It's Michael, isn't it?' He jumped to his feet, took in my body with a quick sweep of his eye and blushed from his neck to the roots of his hair.

'Sorry,' he replied. 'I wasn't going to make you open the door. I didn't mean to embarrass you.'

This was ironic, as I wasn't the one who was embarrassed: I realised that this young man hadn't seen a woman for maybe years, let alone a half-naked one wrapped in a rug. No wonder he was flustered. I pulled the animal skin tighter to me, as he backed away, looking down at his feet.

'I'm afraid your clothes will take another couple of hours to dry, but you're welcome to stay here and walk around the grounds in the meantime. Um, we've called someone to get your car out of the ditch, but they'll have to wait for the floodwaters to subside. So I'm afraid you'll be here at least until late afternoon. Um, I hope that's going to be all right.'

I thanked him and closed the door, unable to stop a giggle at the thought of this innocent young man, so unused to women that the sight of one reduced him to a gibbering wreck.

I ate my breakfast at the window overlooking a peaceful courtyard garden. Every now and then I'd see a hooded figure walking quietly through the cloisters. The silence was wonderful: I couldn't remember the last time I'd felt so much at peace. After an hour or so, I decided to explore. I took a stroll in the grounds, painfully aware of my nudity underneath the simple, hooded robe. I wasn't used to going without a bra, and the bouncing of my breasts without it meant that I was conscious of the curves of my body beneath the shapeless sack. The harsh fabric scratched at my nipples, making them erect. This sign of sexual arousal in such a holy peaceful place was so inappropriate – and that only made them even harder.

The monastery grounds extended for miles. Taking care not to disturb the men who were digging the soil outside, I found a herb garden that was obviously lovingly cultivated and a larger vegetable patch. I observed Michael, his blond hair shining in the weak autumn sun as he worked the land. His sleeves were rolled up and I caught a glimpse of tanned, strong, sinewy forearm.

Inside, I opened various doors and found a refectory, a small kitchen, and a laundry room where my clothes were hanging up on a wooden rack above a heater: tumble dryers obviously hadn't found their way to this place. I felt them: still slightly damp but they'd be dry in another couple of hours. I'd feel better, more in control of myself and my situation when I was back in my own clothes.

My matching crimson lace bra and panties were the only splash of colour in this pale grey room: I thought of Brother Michael rinsing my overtly sexy underwear, couldn't help but picture him bringing my panties to his nose and sniffing . . . I tried to banish the image from my mind.

But the next door I pushed open took my breath away.

It was a stone chamber with a beautiful, sunken pool, the limestone giving the water a greenish, eerie tinge. Light streamed through the slit windows and candles in alcoves lent the whole place an otherworldly appearance. I dipped a toe in the water. It was warm and inviting.

I weighed up the situation. All the men appeared to be engrossed in tasks that would keep them busy for hours. Surely no one would know if I enjoyed a few brief laps? With a quick glance along the corridor to check the coast was clear, I slipped off the robe and lowered myself into the warm, welcoming water. Swimming soothed the muscles that still ached from yesterday's exertions. I'd never swum naked before, let alone in such a calm and beautiful setting, and I loved it, the way the gentle ripples caressed every inch of my body like a lover's hands. My breasts, liberated from underwear or swimsuit, floated attractively on the surface of the water. If the monks got to swim in a place like this every day, no wonder they all looked so serene: it was almost better than sex! I pulled myself out of the water, tiptoed to an alcove where I could peer through a tiny window and check that they were still working outside.

When I turned around and emerged from the alcove, Michael was there. Oblivious to my presence, he shook off his hood and peeled away his robe to reveal a sweaty body now dressed only in plain white underwear. I should have cried out, cleared my throat, anything to make him realise he had an audience but I was dumbstruck by what I saw. I took in a pair of strong, footballer's legs with muscled thighs and a ripped torso. The skin on his arms and faced was ruddy and tanned: the rest of him was smooth, virgin white. I was rooted to the spot, silenced by fear, embarrassment and the fluttering sensation between my legs that always marks the beginning of sexual arousal. With his back to me, he eased his briefs over his hips, revealing a toned, pert arse. I bit my lip, conflicted between wanting to warn him and wanting to see the rest of him.

He stood on the edge of the water, closed his eyes and raised his hands above his head, stretched his body, inhaled deeply. *Then* I saw it all: a dark-blond bush above two pale pink globes hanging either side of an even, uncircumcised penis that was short, thick and chunky. Before diving, he opened his eyes – and of course, that's when he saw me.

He too was shocked into silence and stood there, open mouthed and blinking, like he'd already dived into the water and had swallowed a lungful of water. We remained still, eyes locked, both panicking, neither of us knowing what to say. I was torn between feeling terrible that I'd put him in this position and the thrill of knowing what effect I would be having on him.

By the time his hands went to cover his dick it had already betrayed his reaction to my presence, and was expanding, lengthening out, living up to its full potential. The expression on his face was changing from embarrassment to lust: I had turned him from a spiritual person to flesh and blood, as vulnerable as the rest of us to the forces of desire.

Just the sight of him triggered tiny spasms in my clitoris, but I was the older, experienced person here and I knew that I had to at least try to behave properly. Even if we never touched, I was storing up enough fantasy material to masturbate over for months, I told myself, as I decided that I would take the moral high ground and deny myself – and him – the thing we both most wanted. This place must be rubbing off on me, I thought as I inched my way across the pool room towards the hook where my robe hung. I appear to be developing a conscience!

'I'm sorry,' I said, although I didn't mean it at all. 'It's not fair for me to be in here, and to let you see me like this. If you'll just step aside, I'll take the robe and go back to my room until my clothes are dry.'

I had to walk in his direction. The water cast a flickering green light over everything, including our bodies: aquamarine ripples caressed skin, light bounced off us, giving everything a spookily ethereal quality.

My head told me to keep cool: my body had never burned so hot. With every step I came closer to him, I could feel my heart beat a little faster. My body was betraying me; tits swelling, nipples darkening and becoming more erect. Even if he didn't have enough experience to recognise the classic signs of a highly aroused woman, his dick knew the score. Behind his cupped hands I could see it expanding: he had to keep moving his hands to cover a larger area as it grew and grew.

When I was inches away from him, I could smell the fresh sweat he'd worked up from toiling in the garden: the essential, salty scent of a man who has been at physical work all day. I tried not to inhale too deeply.

I was close enough to reach my robe, if he would only get out of my way. But he didn't: in fact, he stepped to the side, completely blocking my access to it. He looked to the ceiling as if for divine guidance, and then gulped, turned to me and said, 'I've been here since I was sixteen. And I've never had carnal knowledge of a woman.'

He went on, slightly stammering with nerves, or nakedness, or both, 'In three weeks I will take my vows as a monk. Please let me know what it's like before I have to say goodbye to it for ever.'

It was the oddest proposal I'd ever had, and by far the horniest. It was so illicit . . . so wrong . . . so outrageously hot.

'Isn't that forbidden?' I asked, giving him one last chance to save himself.

'It will be in three weeks. But it's not now.'

'I don't know,' I said, the tremor in my voice giving away my internal struggle. 'What if you like it?' (Which I knew he would.) 'What if you leave here because of me? I couldn't be responsible for that.'

My words hung in the air. I guess we could have stayed like that all afternoon, the skinny-dipping journalist and the naked novice monk, debating philosophy and theology on the edge of a sunken pool in rural Wales.

But while I was waiting for an answer, his hand closed over the whole of my breast and softly squeezed it. He was like a child seeing snow for the first time: exploring tentatively, each new sensation bringing a fresh sense of wonder. He then traced a line with his finger down between my breasts and ran his fingers through my pubic hair, combing it gently, a tender, arousing touch that I'd never known from far more experienced lovers. I placed my hand behind his neck and pulled his face down towards mine. Our lips pressed together softly at first, a smooth, dry kiss. By parting my lips I gave him permission to slip his tongue lightly between my teeth and kiss me slowly, indulgently and gently.

I've always believed that a beautiful, tender, sensitive kiss that lasts for just a few seconds is more effective than hours of inept foreplay, and Michael proved my theory right. As his flawless face pressed against mine and our mouths proved to be a perfect fit, my whole body became fluid, yielding. I pressed myself against him, my tits rubbing into the soft fuzz of hair on his muscular chest, his hard-on digging into the softness of my belly, his balls gently resting on my damp pubic hair and twitching as his excitement grew. And as I thought about how young and strong, how inexperienced and innocent he was, and how forbidden what we were doing was, I grew hotter and wetter between my legs.

Now that he'd started, there was no stopping him. He took a step back from me, looked me up and down, his eyes travelling over my body, shedding his innocence like a snakeskin, puppyish enthusiasm darkening into a raw, animal lust.

He bent his head to my breast and began to kiss it with the same beginner's luck he had demonstrated on my mouth, his left hand squeezing my left breast. I leaned back against the stone wall, grateful for its cooling, soothing texture. My whole body throbbed and pulsed under his touch, my clitoris aching for the pressure of his thumb upon it. Instinct can only carry a man so far: I was used to telling much older, more experienced lovers exactly how I needed my clit to be touched. Would he know what my body needed?

Without warning he hooked his hands under my thighs and lifted me as effortlessly as though I were a ragdoll. My tits and belly made contact with the whole of his chest as he lifted me up, up, finally steadying when my pussy was hovering just over his penis. The quivering tip of his hard-on bobbed against my lips.

'Here,' I said, unhooking one arm from around his neck, parting my pussy lips so he could see my clit, pink, erect, damp and desperate for his touch. 'I need you to touch me here.'

I thought that he would bring his hand to my clit but instead he used the tip of his penis to touch and tickle my clitoris. The soft warmth of his dick was a sweet, subtle stimulation that made my whole pussy start to contract. I looked down at his dick: the purple tip was exposed, ultra sensitive, and a tiny pearl of pre-cum oozed from the end. He needed his cock inside me just as much as I did.

Again, I parted my lips with my fingers, exposing my hole, showing him exactly where I needed him to be. He was in me then, driving his big, thick dick into my cunt. The knots of my spine were bruising against the knobbly stone wall. I barely felt it. I buried my head in his chest, inhaled his young, male scent, bit him. This made him thrust harder. I pushed down on his erection with all my bodyweight, feeling him fill me up inside. His pelvic bone jutted out, his bush tickling and teasing my clitoris, sending pre-orgasmic judders throughout my body.

He sank to his knees, strong enough to hold me as he dropped and keep himself inside me. I lay back on the flagstone floor, spread my legs, let him spear me, using all his weight behind it. His body kept up a smooth heave-ho action and not a muscle moved apart from a vein that stood out on his face. I lost control of mine and turned into an animal. I wriggled underneath him, dug my heels into his arse. I clawed at his back, miaowed like a cat, while he grunted in time to his pounding thrusts. My tits jiggled, my arse shook as I rubbed against him, harder, faster, not caring about anything but what I was doing to him and what he was doing to me.

When I came, I pushed my fingers into his firm buttocks, wanting him deeper and deeper into me. The whole-body spasms were more intense and longer than any other I'd ever had, a series of tiny explosions in my body; just when I thought the bomb had been detonated another blast would rip through me, overwhelming me again. My orgasm massaged Michael's hard dick as it moved inside me: he came too, pleasure and guilt washing over on his features as his spunk shot into me. We lay together in the light of the poolside, the lapping of the water and his deep breathing were the only noise. Eventually, we rolled apart.

Brother Michael waded into the pool, immersed himself in the water. I joined him. His cum floated out of my pussy, the silky liquid making a faint white marble pattern on the surface of the water.

'So,' I said. 'What now?'

'I don't know,' he said, looking at the milky liquid instead of meeting my eyes, suddenly the gauche novice again. 'I feel that it's going to take a lot more than this pool to cleanse me after that. But thank you,' he said, pulling me to him. 'You've given me a wonderful experience. It's up to me now what I decide. Please, you mustn't feel any guilt.'

I kissed him goodbye, raised myself out of the water and wrapped my damp body in the oversized robe. I could feel his eyes boring into my back as I walked out of the pool room, but I didn't look back. I don't think you ever should. I exchanged my robe for my own clothes on the way back to my chamber: they were still a little damp, but the heat from my body would dry them out in no time. I was met in the corridor by the kind old monk who'd opened the door for me yesterday.

'Ah, there you are,' he said. 'The breakdown services are waiting to take you to your car. I do hope you get back to London safely.' I thanked him for his hospitality and walked out of the monastery and back into real life.

To this day, I don't know whether Brother Michael

took his vows or left holy orders for a new life that included sex. Part of me hopes he's still there. It's not often you can say you were a man's first *and* last.

MASQUERADE

In my last collection, I printed a story about supermodel 'Anna Lamb' and her rock star boyfriend Joey, told to me by a mutual friend. I had every journalist in London begging me to reveal her true identity. I refused, of course.

Word got back to me that Anna was thrilled with the story and got off in it being shared with so many others. I would never risk unmasking Anna; not only has she become a friend, but also one who trusts me and I couldn't live without hearing her stories. This one was so steamy that I played the tape of her voice back before bed every night for a week and Anna's more than happy for you to hear her confession too . . .

Anna Lamb was bored. Joey Harper, her lover, and *enfant terrible* of the British music scene, was on tour in Canada and she was stuck on a modelling assignment in Hawaii. When he toured, all the creativity Joey usually channelled into their sex life was focused on his stage performance, and Anna was feeling lonely and neglected. She was used to Joey thinking up wild, creative sex games for them to play, each adventure more daring than the last.

But it had been a whole month since their last fuck, a memorable occasion where he'd ravished her backstage in her dressing room during Milan fashion week. They'd talked about it on the phone of course, reliving the experience, but there was only so much time you could spend with one hand holding your mobile and the other down your pants. Anna kept Joey on the ball – and distracted him from the attention of a legion of teenage fans – by sending him explicit phone messages, videos of her body, the camera slowly panning down a bikini top to reveal a tiny, tanned breast, a strand of dirty-blonde hair brushing her shoulder, her tight, exquisite pussy – she was quite the supermodel *all* over. Anna may have been one of the most photographed women in the world, but these short films were for Joey's eyes only.

Anna's boredom was replaced by excitement on the evening her modelling assignment finished. Her phone vibrated and beeped: Joey had sent her a text message.

'Got a couple of days off. Need a fuck. Get to LA tomorrow night. Meet me at the Sunset Bar at 10 p.m. xxx'

Any of the millionaire playboys Anna had dated before she met Joey would have chartered her a flight, or come to pick her up in person. Joey issued the orders and left her to fly halfway across America to meet him under her own steam. And that was exactly why Anna liked him. This skinny rock urchin was the only man she'd ever met who had the confidence – well, the arrogance really – to treat her not as a fragile sculpture to be placed on a pedestal and worshipped, but as a sex object to indulge his every perversion. It never occurred to Joey that Anna would say no. That was his appeal: well, that and his nimble, skilled musician's fingers and a dick so big that every fuck felt like a deflowering thought Anna, with a secret smile.

Twenty-four hours, a few frantic phone calls and a lot of credit card payments later, Anna was picked up by a chauffeur from LAX airport. She checked into her pristine white suite at the trendy, minimalist Sunset Hotel at 8 p.m: she was due to meet Joey in the exclusive bar, for hotel guests and A-list superstars only, in exactly two hours.

She took a shower and leisurely tidied her bikini line, shaving her pubic hair down to just a tiny strip, the size and shape of a plectrum, a couple of centimetres above her clitoris. She could feel the sensitive bud swelling in anticipation of Joey's visit: as she soaped herself, she trailed her fingers along the nearly-nude mound. Idly, she wondered if she should keep stroking, part her pussy lips, expose her clit and touch herself. On the one hand, if she came now, she would be a little more cool and calm when she met Joey, not so desperate for sex that she'd let him do just anything to her. On the other, she was already building up a delicious knot of sexual tension. She knew from past experience that when Joey finally permitted her to release it, it would make for an even more intense orgasm. She whipped her fingers away from her clit: hold out for pleasure, she thought. Wait for him.

Anna left her blonde hair tousled the way Joey liked it and wore no make-up apart from the black kohl eyeliner that was her trademark. She slid her naked body into a second-skin red minidress and checked herself out in the mirror: she looked good. She wore no underwear: what was the point? It never stayed on for long when Joey was around, and he liked to be able to access her pussy wherever they were, no matter that they might be caught with his hand up her skirt.

It was 9.55 p.m. She was due to meet Joey downstairs in five minutes. She cracked open a bottle of champagne, strode out on to her balcony and lit a cigarette. Smoking in LA is virtually banned outright these days, but what the fuck. She took a deep drag, felt the nicotine and champagne hit her bloodstream, giddy and light-headed with anticipation as she looked out over the Hollywood Hills.

At 10.40 p.m. Anna sauntered down to the Sunset Bar, expecting Joey to be waiting for her. She ordered herself a Kir Royale – they did the best champagne cocktails in the world at the Sunset – and scoured the room for him. He wasn't there. She surveyed her fellow drinkers. The women and men in here were identikit: perfect blonde highlights, perfect capped teeth, perfect nose jobs, perfect tans. Perfectly dull, thought Anna. Not one of the built-up hunks in here possessed an ounce of scruffy little Joey's sex appeal.

At 11 p.m. he arrived. Anna saw him in the doorway and gasped, as struck now by his unique sex appeal as she was the first time she'd laid eyes him. He wore skinny black jeans and a dirty, loose, black pirate-style muslin shirt, open to his skinny waist. Love beads hung around his neck, caressing his nipples, and black leather bands decorated his wrists: the black nail varnish on his fingers was chipped and he wore old, scuffed baseball boots on his feet. When he saw Anna he didn't say hello, didn't apologise for being late, simply walked over to her, leant in and kissed her, his tongue exploring her as though she was a brand-new woman instead of one that he knew every inch of, inside and out.

'Hey, baby,' he said. Never apologise, never explain. How ridiculously arousing she found his arrogance. 'Let's get out of here. This place gives me the creeps.'

'We can't leave! You've only just got here! I haven't finished my drink!'

Joey grabbed the cocktail from Anna's hand, downed it in one.

'You have now. I'm going, with or without you.'

He was right, of course. Anna, the supermodel whose fiery temper had once been the stuff of tabloid legend, the girl who ate men for breakfast, meekly followed Joey out of the bar and to the hotel forecourt where a driver was waiting for them in a big black Mercedes with tinted windows. Anna felt a pang of frustration: Joey's idea of nightlife often involved hanging out with other bands, which invariably led to some after-show party in a grimy basement club with a sticky floor and hundreds of groupies who won't let a little thing like a supermodel girlfriend come between them and their idol.

But more than that, she wanted to be alone with Joey. The way he'd kissed her in the hotel bar had set off a chain reaction of desire, first in her lips, then her breasts, down her body and culminating in a throbbing, burning pussy and clit that would ache with frustration until she felt Joey touch her there. If they were partying with other celebs and hangers-on, it would be dawn before they got to crawl into her big white bed and fuck: and she couldn't wait that long, she just couldn't.

'How was last night's gig?' she said to Joey as they slid across the leather seats of the car.

'Okay,' he said, pulling her close to his chest. 'Had a massive hard-on thinking about you right through the set. Gave my music an extra charge. Nearly had a wank over the thought of you but I thought I'd save myself for tonight.'

He rested his hand casually between Anna's legs, bare and exposed in her miniskirt. The finger that he used for strumming his guitar and had a little rough skin on it was also the one he'd used so many times to tickle and tease her to orgasm. Was he going to fuck or finger her in the back of this car? She would let him, of course she would, she had no choice. She was so overcome with lust she almost wanted him to bring her off right there . . . but that was a little tame by Joey's standards. If that was all he could manage after a month apart, then he was losing his touch.

Joey's hand remained motionless, the intense chemistry between he and Anna could do far more to arouse her than any touch ever could. If he felt the moisture beginning to trickle out of her pussy and stain her dress he didn't remark on it. As the car sped through the wide LA streets, the landscape changed: the grand boutiques, mansions and restaurants gave way to shabby apartment blocks, boarded-up stores and burnt-out cars. In this sinister new environment, Joey began to relax and enjoy himself. He smiled as he reached under his seat and handed Anna a black pouch.

'Open it,' he said. Intrigued, Anna pulled at the bag's little velvet ribbon drawstrings and pulled out a dazzling gold mask, like one worn at a Venice ball: opulently decorated with bronze feathers, it covered her eyes and nose, but left her pointed chin and rosebud pout on display.

'What's this for?' said Anna, no longer bored. 'And where are we going?'

'In answer to your first question, this is so that no one will recognise you. As to where we're going . . . I'm taking you on a new adventure, baby. One you'll never forget. I've found a *very* exclusive club and you wouldn't believe what I had to do to get us membership for one night only.'

'A club?' Anna couldn't hide her disappointment and wriggled in her seat, trying to rub her clit against Joey's hand, encouraging him to stroke her in response, but he took his fingers away and tapped on the glass separating them from the driver. 'Thanks mate . . . next turning on the left, please.' The car suddenly exited the boulevard and crawled down a dim, scruffy alleyway. This was nothing like the fabulous, glossy side of LA that Anna knew. She was aware that there was an underground rock 'n' roll scene in the city, but an exclusive club in *this* location defied belief. In Anna's experience, exclusive clubs tended to be on brightly lit avenues with red carpets and velvet ropes.

'Wait here, mate,' said Joey, handing the driver a roll of money. 'I dunno when we'll be out. Could be a long one. Then again,' he said, with a conspiratorial wink, 'The missus might not like it. Might see you again in five minutes.'

Before they left the car, Joey said to Anna, 'Keep your mask on. This place is so secret there shouldn't be any paparazzi or undercover journalists but you never know.' With real tenderness, he tied the mask a little tighter around Anna's eyes, fastening it behind her head with a sturdy knot. The ribbon brushed against her shoulders and collarbone, a sensual echo of Joey's caress. She closed her eyes, enjoyed the soft brushing of silk on her skin. When she looked at Joey again, he was wearing a black Zorro mask; his too covered the eyes but stopped short of the sexy sneer Anna adored. 'Oh . . . great,' said Anna, faking enthusiasm for Joey's bizarre costume, trying to hide a stab of disappointment. But they wouldn't be alone at a club. They'd have to shake off groupies and end up fucking in the toilets. (Anna had now reached the point where orgasm within the next couple of hours was a physical necessity, not an option.) And while cubicle sex could be hot, horny and urgent . . . well, they'd been there, done that, too.

With one hand on the door handle, Joey slid his guitar finger up along the inside of Anna's taut, toned thigh and deep into her pussy, evidence that he'd known all along just how turned on she was. He twisted his finger inside her, bent it at the knuckle, found her G-spot and rubbed his fingertip against it before withdrawing and then slipping the juice-slicked finger slowly into his own mouth. They stepped out of the air-conditioned cab into the warmth of the LA evening, Anna in her red dress and gold mask and Joey in head-to-toe black, two anonymous clubbers.

The car pulled away to park just out of sight around a corner. All that was visible of the club from the road was an unremarkable black door in a shabby two-storey building. A burly security guard wearing a headset was the only person in the street.

He looked Joey up and down.

'Can I take your name, sir?'

'Joey Harper', said Joey. The bouncer said something into his earpiece, listened to a voice and then nodded.

'Password?'

'Masquerade,' said Joey.

The black door swung open and they entered the club that didn't even have a name.

It took a while for Anna's eyes to adjust to the darkness inside. The walls and floor were black but the ceiling was mirrored and studded with tiny lights that cast an eerie glow over everything. In the half-dark, Anna could see groups of three or four people snuggled in booths. It wasn't particularly warm – the air-con was turned on full, Anna was used to humid, sweaty dancefloors with strobes and flashing coloured lights and well-lit areas entrances for the A-list to pose in Dolce, de la Renta, Marchesa, for authorised gossip-mag paps – and for each other. Most of the clientele in here seemed to be dressed in high-end beachwear, frowned Anna, despite the fact that she, at least, had goosebumps along her fine limbs. Nestled in one alcove she thought she saw the dim, blurred outline of a pair of large, round breasts but when she looked again, the figure disappeared.

Black-painted partitions and walls divided the club into a series of secluded areas, saloon seats, cubby-holes, private booths, and alcoves. It felt more like a secret labyrinth than a nightclub. Holes at intervals in some of the walls let chinks of dim light shine through from a dancefloor. This was empty but for a young woman wearing a Swarovski-crystal-studded bikini, a pair of knee-high boots and a mask not unlike Anna's. Joey took Anna's hand firmly and led her across the dancefloor. What she saw at the other end of the room made her stop in her tracks.

On a raised platform was a huge deep-red bed, the mattress covered in scarlet silk, framed by wine-coloured velvet drapes. It was more appropriate for the boudoir of a seventeenth-century French king than a club in LA. It was the most brightly lit thing in the room: dripping candles in ornate candelabras cast a sexy, flickering glow over everything.

But the really remarkable thing was not the bed itself, but the spectacle taking place upon it. A man in a full-face black leather mask and a pair of biker boots, lay back on the bed. His long blond hair poked out through the bottom of the mask, and his tongue lolled through a tiny zipper that allowed access to his mouth. A pair of identical twins were his companions: naked except for platform, Perspex-soled, pole-dancer's heels and large hoop earrings, these girls had Hollywood tans and platinum blonde hair, set in soft Marilyn Monroe-style waves. One of the girls was on her knees, straddling the man's legs at the knee – her head busy at his large, solid penis. This latter-day Norma Jean sucked hard, her mouth, slicked with vermilion lipstick, moving up and down over the quivering hard-on. Her make-up made a red ring around the base of his cock and her pink tongue and even white teeth were occasionally visible. Her high round tits, so perfect they had to be the work of an extremely skilled plastic surgeon, brushed against his thighs as his body bucked and arched underneath her. Now that Anna looked more closely, she could see that they weren't in fact twins, but two similar-looking beautiful girls milking a classic male fantasy for all it was worth. The other blonde knelt over the man's face, daring him to taste her pussy but permitting him only occasional laps at her juicy cunt. She too wore the red lips and black eye make-up of a 1950s starlet and as he struggled to make contact with her slit she threw back her pretty head and laughed, delighted with the effect her teasing had on her plaything.

Anna was shocked and excited. Until now, her experiences with Joey had been strictly one-on-one. Sure, they'd taken their chances and fucked in public more than once, but they'd never been so close to other people doing it in front of them. How clever of Joey to find this place! And how fucking horny she was!

'Well,' said Joey, taking a glass of champagne offered by a passing waiter, who was naked but for an apron. 'What do you think?'

'I'm lost for words,' said Anna, and her voice took on the low, gravelly tone it always did when she was aroused but trying to control herself. 'What is this place? And who *are* all these people?'

'People like you and me, my darling,' said Joey. 'Famous, successful people who want to explore their sexuality and have a little fun but would prefer that fact kept out of the papers.'

Right then the man on the bed came, shooting an arc of white spunk into the mouth of one of his blonde companions. She pursed her red lips together, letting a string of cum leak from the corner of her mouth. The two identical girls then knelt opposite each other over the man's prone and shuddering body, and kissed deeply, passing his fluid back and forth between their mouths as his erection slowly ebbed: when another drop of cum leaked out of the tip of his diminishing hard-on, the girls play-fought over it. They pulled each other's curls and slapped each other's tits and giggled as their mouths battled for access to his cock. Anna, who had never thought of herself as lesbian, had never seen anything so erotic in her life. She felt a familiar warm moisture trickle down the inside of her own leg: God, she was soaking.

She reached a hand round and slid it into Joey's skinny jeans: he was hard all right, the jutting rod of his dick trapped inside the tight denim. Anna used her fingers to circle and twist around the top of his penis, just the way he liked it. He let out a low moan of pleasure, the first sign he'd given all evening that he felt just as horny as she.

One Marilyn began to dribble, from her beautiful pout, a thin stream of the man's semen on to the other's breasts and she in turn responded likewise, the two massaged cum into each other. Now that he had recovered, the masked man sat up and joined in, sucking first one girl's nipple and then the other, tasting his own liquid on skin. As he twisted his body, he revealed a heavily tattooed back with an instantly recognisable piece of body-art. The name of a prominent Hollywood actress was scrolled in elaborate gothic lettering across both his shoulder blades. Anna let out a gasp of revelation: the actress was married to a famous singer, she had a corresponding design bearing his name on her shoulder. The couple were notorious for their matching tattoos and for going under the needle together every anniversary. Needless to say, neither of the mini-Marilyns was the rock star's spouse.

Joey threw his head back and laughed, almost scornfully as he saw recognition dawning on Anna's face.

'Now you see why we all have to wear the masks in here, my love?' he said. 'That's a career-ending and marriage-wrecking experience for him if it ever got out.'

Anna sat on a plush purple bench with Joey and watched the scene unfold. Now that she knew what kind of place she was in, she realised that every other person in the club was a household name on five continents: that woman there in the peacock-feather mask could hide her face but her lean frame and long, auburn curls could only belong to a one-time teenage movie star who'd made her millions playing sweet, innocent girl-next-door characters. What would people say if they could see her now, with one dick in her mouth and another up her arse? Anna wondered if anyone had recognised her. She half-hoped that they could.

The sight of the red-haired woman tipped Anna over the edge: she needed to fuck and she needed it now. She turned to kiss Joey, happy for him to go as far as he wanted in this place where, clearly, anything went. He kissed her back, softly at first and then more voraciously. He pulled down the lycra fabric of her dress so that one small breast was exposed: her nipple was rock-hard, and the softness of Joey's lips on it felt like heaven. Finally her body was receiving the same level of physical stimulation she'd just visually enjoyed. He sucked harder than he had ever done before, drawing out her breast with his teeth then letting it spring back to her body. The harder he sucked, the more engorged Anna's clit became. She guided his hand down to her pussy, aching for him to caress her there, but Joey had other ideas.

'Not here . . .' he whispered, gesturing to the dance-floor. 'I want to touch you through the wall.'

What did he mean? Anna didn't know, but nodded her head in meek acquiescence anyway. Joey led her to a tiny booth with two screens about seven foot high on either side. If you looked closely you could see holes at face, hip and breast level.

'Stay there,' commanded Joey. Anna stood between the two screens, then her lover disappeared. She stayed frozen for a few seconds, unsure as to what was about to happen next but certain it would be something exciting. Looking down, she saw a familiar male hand wearing chipped black nail varnish reach through a hole level with her tits. The groping hand pulled down her tube dress to reveal her breasts, the light-brown nipples swollen and hard. Another hand appeared lower-down and ruthlessly yanked her hem up, displaying her swollen pussy lips, bald expect for that tiny plectrum-shaped patch of hair above her clitoris.

A crowd of people gathered in front of them to see this beautiful body. People in Hollywood are used to physical perfection, but few of them had ever seen a body as magnetically attractive as Anna's: the pert little tits, the peachy skin, the flawless arse, the legs that went on for ever, from her tidy, fleshy pussy to her silky, elegant feet. And this was a body that was clearly horny as hell and more than ready for sex: Anna moved slowly and sensuously as Joey's disembodied hands explored, tweaked and caressed her. She'd never been more turned on in her life, and although her mask hid the expressions of ecstasy on her face, her arousal showed.

Anna closed her eyes, abandoned herself to the sensation of Joey's touch. She wiggled and writhed as hands came and went on both sides, pinching her tits, forcing a finger between her lips so she could bite down on it, even pushing an open palm flat against her throat so that she felt dizzy and light-headed. She felt two fingers either side of her clitoris, slipping into her pussy to use her natural juices as a lubricant for fast, firm rubbing on her hard, swollen bud. It was heaven: she could feel the heat building in her pussy as she enjoyed the sensations: a hand on each breast, pulling the nipples out, pulling them up, around and down, shaking her tits like jellies, plus a third finger rubbing furiously at her clit –

Anna opened her eyes and looked down. Three hands! Three hands, moving so fast that she couldn't tell whose they were. They couldn't all be Joey's, so who was the other person? She looked out into the crowd of spectators. A group of twenty or so people had gathered around. Most were fondling their partners or touching themselves. There, at the front of the group, fly unzipped, dick in hand, was Joey, staring at her through his mask, a lusty sneer curling his top lip. So whose hands were these that were bringing her to the brink of orgasm? And when had Joey orchestrated the changeover?

She thrust her hips backwards, pulled her clit away from a probing hand: she could relax, let go and have strangers bring her to orgasm, but she didn't want to come unless Joey was inside her. The hands on her breasts kept up their steady movements Was that ruby-red nail varnish? Female fingers? A *woman* rubbing me to orgasm? thought Anna as she squinted at a delicate hand in the fuzzy blur of half-light and sensory overload With a massive effort, Anna tore herself away from the caresses and approached Joey, wrapped her fingers around his dick, squeezed hard.

Her dress was still around her waist like a thick red belt. She didn't bother to cover herself up. What was the point? They'd seen everything now. And it felt good, having her tits and arse exposed to the breeze of the air-con. As she led Joey to the dancefloor, male and female hands reached out to touch her. How many of these people knew they were feeling up Anna Lamb, supermodel, society girl, pin-up, party animal, *sex slave*?

The once-empty dancefloor was now packed. People danced in twos, threes and fours, naked people pressed up close to fully and fabulously dressed companions. But Anna only wanted one dance partner. In her heels, she was an inch or two taller than Joey. She parted her legs and he let the tip of his hard-on bounce against her pussy lips, teasing herself as much as him. Slow hip-hop music played softly in the background.

'You bastard,' she said, but the smile on her face told him she had loved every second of her experience. 'You'd have let me come there, thinking it was you.'

'Yes,' said Joey, and his breath tasted of Jack Daniels and rock 'n' roll. 'It doesn't matter how hard you come. I can *always* make you come again.'

'But I'm horny *now*,' said Anna, like a spoilt child. 'I'm ready *now*. Please don't make me wait until we go back to the hotel. I want to fuck you *here*. Now! '

'You'll come when I say,' said Joey, asserting his

authority. 'And you'll also come where I say,' he said, his gaze travelling up to the velvet-draped bed.

'I couldn't!' said Anna reflexively, although as soon as the words were out she knew that she could and she would. Joey turned her around and pushed her towards the bed, his hard-on nestling into the small of her back.

Once on the bed, he took off her shoes and gently rolled her dress down over her ankles. Anna tugged at Joey's shirt and ripped it off him: he kept his beads and wristbands on but wriggled out of his drainpipe jeans to reveal a lean white arse and a hard-on that was anything *but* skinny sticking bolt-upright from under a dark brown thatch of pubic hair.

They were naked and tangled up together within seconds. The two masked figures made an arresting picture on the bed: the perfect blonde in the golden mask, and the pale, lanky guy hovering over her with a massive erection.

Anna spread her legs and waited for him to spear the cock she so adored into her. But instead, he plucked one of the thick, church-style candles that surrounded the bed from its candelabra, held it aloft and tilted it, dripping wax all over Anna's tits and belly. She screamed in surprise, then with pain, and finally with excitement. The hot wax sizzling against skin that was already highly sensitised made her feel alive. Alive and awake and aware of every inch of her body. Joey trailed the candle down the centre of her body, letting the wax pool and harden just above her pubic bone. Anna was torn between thrill and terror. He was dangerously close to her clitoris. Would Joey be cruel enough to burn that part's most tender, delicate skin? And yet, and yet . . . after such a prolonged and frustrating build-up of sexual tension, she almost wanted to experience pain right on her clit just so she could feel a sensation of *some* (any!) kind down there . . .

Joey didn't drip wax on Anna's clit but what he did do next shocked everyone in the audience, Anna included. He blew on the candle to extinguish it, sending flecks of burning wax all over Anna's body. He put it into his mouth to cool it down, and then slowly, slowly began to push it inside her. As soon as she realised what he was doing, she spread her legs even wider, eager to be filled by something so thick and solid. The sturdy waxy cylinder forced Anna's cunt open, stretched her wider than she'd ever been opened before. It felt so good to have something inside her at last. She fantasised that the cold, clammy wax was Joey's dick. He left the candle inside her while he went to work on the rest of her body. Every single person on the dancefloor was standing, watching, masturbating, and Anna waited patiently while Joey peeled off all the wax that had set and hardened on her body. Each piece he removed tore away with it fine downy hairs on her skin, making it even more painful coming off than it had been going on. When Joey came up to remove some of the wax on Anna's tits and collarbone, he bent down and whispered into her ear, 'Well done, baby. You're doing really well,' he said, and he slid his forefinger, rough and calloused from years of guitar playing, on to her clitoris and pressed down hard. Anna whimpered. 'I'm going to let you come soon: I thought you would have already. I'm gonna fuck you so hard it's gonna happen in seconds. My balls are huge, I've got loads of spunk to shoot into you.'

With one final twist of the wax cylinder, Joey removed it from the model's pussy and placed it at the front of the stage. A man dressed in a formal business suit made a grab for the candle and started licking it. That's the closest you'll ever get to tasting me, thought Anna. I'm never fucking anyone else but Joey. Never!

And then at last, at long fucking last, Joey gave Anna what she craved: propping himself up on skinny, tattooed forearms, he drove his dick into her yearning cunt. It was hot and throbbing compared to the cool smoothness of the candle. He remained motionless, letting his erection get harder and thicker inside her. Anna moved under him, grinding her clit against his pubic bone. She thrashed beneath him as if an electric charge flowed violently through her body as she rubbed faster and faster against him. Her orgasm ripped through her like a typhoon, obliterating all other thoughts and feelings, making her legs convulse and her cunt pulsate more intensely than she'd ever known it before.

As she surrendered to her orgasm, the ribbons on Anna's mask begin to unravel. In the final throes of her climax, the mask slipped, and for one brief second the clientele of the club with no name saw the million-dollar face of Anna Lamb, supermodel, as she lost control of her perfect features. Anna clutched at the mask and held it to her face again. She'd only been exposed for a few seconds, but what crucial few seconds they had been! She lifted her pelvis, pressed her legs together, knowing it would trigger Joey's orgasm. He came hard, his rock 'n' roll singer's voice hitting a high note that was as recognisable in its own way to his fans as Anna's face was to hers. When he finally collapsed on her, she wrapped her legs around his back and lifted her head; he made sure her mask was secure before he raised her from the bed and dressed her with a tenderness that made a beautiful contrast to the torture he could dish out when he wanted to. He rolled the tube dress back on to her exhausted body, pulled the jeans up over his still-hard cock. His torn shirt he used to wipe up the traces of spunk on the bed, and then threw it over the crowd where three half-dressed women began fighting for it.

Anna and Joey looked at the crowd. They'd both given

the performance of their lives that night. There was no way they'd ever top it. Exhilarated, but now exhausted too, they linked arms and ran out of the club. Shoes in hand, they scampered along the dim corridor, past the bouncer and through the door into warm, dry air that wrapped them up like a blanket. The couple rounded a corner and jumped into the waiting car. The only sign they had ever been there were two masks, one golden, one black, tossed carelessly on to the tarmac of the LA street.